John Hannibal Sheppard

Memoir of Marshall P. Wilder

John Hannibal Sheppard

Memoir of Marshall P. Wilder

ISBN/EAN: 9783337382391

Printed in Europe, USA, Canada, Australia, Japan

Cover: Foto ©Andreas Hilbeck / pixelio.de

More available books at **www.hansebooks.com**

MEMOIR

OF

MARSHALL P. WILDER.

BY

JOHN H. SHEPPARD, A.M.

LIBRARIAN.

[From the New England Historical and Genealogical Register for April, 1867.]

BOSTON:

DAVID CLAPP & SON, PRINTERS......334 WASHINGTON STREET.

1867.

MARSHALL PINCKNEY WILDER.

To portray the life and labors of one so widely known, and so intimately connected by numerous official relations with public institutions and the great industrial enterprises of the age, is an arduous and responsible task ; more especially as several sketches of this distinguished Horticulturist have already appeared, and a fresh memorial of his life, though extending to a later period and containing many facts which are found in no other narrative, may lack the charm of originality. Col. Wilder has long been an honored member of the New England Historic-Genealogical Society, and it was by the request of the Committee of Publication that he kindly, though reluctantly, consented to allow us the use of his Portrait* for this number of the Register. For it is the province and object of this Society to obtain biographies of benefactors of our country ; and if possible, while they are living, to treasure up and record the events of their lives, before it is too late and they are lost forever.

Marshall Pinckney Wilder was born September 22, 1798, at Rindge in New Hampshire ; he is the oldest son of Samuel Locke Wilder, Esq., and his grandmother was sister of Samuel Locke, D.D., former President of Harvard University, from whom his father derived his Christian name. With an elder brother his father removed, in 1794, to Rindge, from Sterling, anciently a part of Lancaster, Massachusetts, where they commenced business as merchants. He was representative to the New Hampshire Legislature thirteen years, held important offices, and was a member of the Congregational Church of

---

* This excellent likeness is from a fine steel engraving, formerly executed in connection with his services while President of the American Pomological and the United States Agricultural Societies.

2

that place. He married Miss Anna Sherwin, May 2, 1797—a lady endeared to her friends by great moral worth and piety, and a warm admirer of the beauties of nature. They had four sons and five daughters. In the Indian wars, to which the border settlements were peculiarly exposed, and in the Revolution and Shays's rebellion, the paternal ancestors of Col. Wilder performed meritorious services; and his grandfather was one of the seven delegates from Worcester County, in the Convention of Massachusetts, 1787, who voted in favor of the Constitution of the United States. The Worcester Magazine, Vol. ii. p. 45, bears this testimony :—" Of all the ancient Lancaster families, there is no one that has sustained so many important offices as that of Wilder."

Rindge was incorporated in 1768, and has given birth to several men who rose to a high rank in society. It lies six miles to the south of Monadnock, and in the midst of hills and forests, with thirteen ponds in its embrace. It possesses all the charm of a rural village, surrounded by picturesque scenery. From one of the heights may be traced streams, which from one declivity run into the Merrimack, and on the opposite side into the Connecticut. Rindge was famous in the Revolution for the daring and patriotism of its citizens ; for hardly had the news of the battle of Lexington reached their ears, before a company of fifty men was organized, equipped and sent off in defence of their country ; three of whom fell at Bunker Hill. The population of the place in 1859—according to Coolidge's valuable " History and Description of New England "—was only 1274. But it should be recollected that many a beautiful and flourishing town in that State has been merely the birth-place and nursery of young men who, when their education was finished, like fledged birds leaving the maternal nest, emigrated to some larger and more enterprising place. The granite hills of New Hampshire abound with such instances, producing minds like the diamond of the first water. Who can forget Edward Payson, the eloquent divine ; Lewis Cass, Levi Woodbury, Jeremiah Mason, or that man of massive intellect, Daniel Webster, who seemed to wield the artillery of Heaven in the thunders of his eloquence ! What a host of eminent men were born and nurtured among the highlands of New Hampshire !

Such was the birth-place of the subject of this memoir. From the door-step of his father's house he could gaze, on a summer morn, on hills and valleys, on flocks and herds, and the abodes of industry and comfort ; or here, too, by a short ascent, he could behold the majestic Monadnock, which from its throne in the air looks down upon a hundred smiling villages—a mountain from whose summit may be seen the White Hills, Ascutney and Wachusett, looming up on the verge of the horizon, and afar off a dim view of Boston and the ocean.

That such rural charms and sublime scenes in childhood had an influence on his future career, there can be no doubt ; for his favorite pursuits in life and his numerous speeches on public occasions are imbued with an enthusiastic love of Nature. Indeed, the brain of a child is a busy workshop. The philosopher may study it, but he cannot enter into the mysterious working of the boy's mind and predict with certainty what the man may be hereafter. The turn for a particular pursuit—the tact for some invention or discovery—the talent to charm the world by some heroic act, or intellectual power, may lie for years in embryo, until time or opportunity call it forth.

" It may be a sound—
A tone of music—summer's eve—or spring—
A flower—the wind—the ocean—which shall wound,
Striking the electric chain, wherewith we are darkly bound."—BYRON.

The parents of young Marshall well knew the value and importance of education, and they sent him to school, at the early age of four years. That period and his school-boy days Mr. Wilder has described to us in a speech which he made on the 14th of November, 1861. It was on the Fortieth Anniversary of the pastorate of the Rev. A. W. Burnham, D.D. ; at the celebration of which, several of the sons of Rindge, who had long been residents in other places, were present. After Dr. B. had delivered an appropriate discourse at the church before a large audience, the assembly adjourned to the town hall, decorated for the festival, and partook of a handsome collation. The presiding officer, S. B. Sherwin, Esq., then called on the speakers, and the floods of memory began to break forth in sweet reminiscences of boyhood. Mr. Wilder drew a graphic picture of his early life, wherein he portrayed the old school-house near his father's door—the little rods of chastisement "resembling a bundle of apple grafts," behind the master's desk, and the evening spelling matches, where each one carried a candle in a turnip to the arena. The whole description is so true to nature, and given in so humorous and happy a manner, that it is to be regretted that only a few extracts can be given.

"Who," said he, "that has a soul within him can forget the place of his birth, the home of his childhood, the old District School where he learned his A B C, the Church where he was offered at the baptismal font, or the consecrated ground in which repose the loved and lost ones of earth?"

Touching his studies, and he had already gone through Adams's arithmetic, he quotes a quaint verse—some old college dithyrambic—

"Multiplication is vexation,
Division is as bad;
The Rule of Three, it puzzles me,
And Fractions make me mad."

"Well, Sir, here I finished my common school education, and entered upon a higher course of study, which my venerable father—God be thanked that he is spared to this day—hoped would terminate in one of the learned professions. And strange as it may seem, I proceeded so far, as to read six or seven books of the Æneid of Virgil; and now, lest any one should doubt the correctness of this statement, I will attempt to construe and translate a line which I have not seen since that time. It ran thus :—'Musa,' Oh *muse;* 'memora,' *declare;* 'mihi,' *to me;* 'causas,' *the causes;* ' quo numine læso '—Ah, Mr. President, my memory falters, and I shall leave it to the learned divines by my side to translate the three last words." (Laughter). He goes on, "I think, however, I can truly say, that from the day my sainted mother first took me into the garden, 'to help dress and to keep it,' I have never seen the time when I did not love the cultivation of the soil, and I shall never cease to feel that a part of my humble mission on earth is to promote that most honorable and useful of all employments."

He speaks affectionately of "his honored Pastor," and goes on :

"I can recollect this old Church as it then was, with its high pulpit, spacious galleries and its square pews, surmounted with a balustrade, and rail, and how terrified I was if by chance I turned one of the rounds and made it squeak, lest I should have disturbed the venerable Deacon Blake, whose pew was between that of my father and the sacred desk; and now and then in time of service I opened one eye and looked around to espy the handsomest young lady in the congregation; and that here it was my eye caught hers, who became my first love and the wife of my youth. Of one other circumstance I have been reminded to-day by our honored Pastor, namely, that forty years ago this day I acted as chorister at his ordination."

These quotations need no apology. They seem like photographs of long buried friends; they bring back the halcyon days of boyhood, and must call up many delightful recollections to every one who feels that the finger of time has touched his brow. And who that ever felt grief, would not sympathize with him, when he said :

"I never return to this good old town—the place of my birth, the home of my youth, and in whose sacred soil repose my mother, my brother and sister, the wife of my youth, and some of my children—but I feel sensations which no language can describe. I never revisit this ancient town, but with the first glimpse of her glorious old hills, over which I have roamed in my youth with gun and fishing rod, my soul rises with the inspiration of the scene, and I almost involuntarily exclaim, 'Thank God, I am with you once again!'

> 'I feel the gales that from ye blow,
> A momentary bliss bestow,
> As waving fresh your gladsome wing
> My buoyant soul you seem to soothe,
> And redolent with scenes of youth,
> I breathe a second spring.' "

At the age of twelve he was sent to New Ipswich Academy, under the care of Master Taylor. At this seminary, which was founded in 1789, several men of distinction received their early education : among whom were S. P. Miles, late principal of the High School, Boston ; Rev. Addison Searle, Chaplain in U. S. Navy ; the late Dr. Augustus A. Gould, and others, a sketch of whom will be found in the account of the Academy by Frederic Kidder, Esq., in the History of New Ipswich. He was there one year, and returning home he was put under the tuition of the Rev. Joseph Brown, it being his father's wish that he should receive a collegiate education and pursue some profession. But Providence otherwise ordered. With his gun and fishing rod, he preferred the forests and lakes of his native place and an active life, to all the charms of Virgil, though teaching the woodlands to resound ever so sweetly with the beautiful Amaryllis. Whatever his studies were, or the books he read at that time, he certainly did lay the foundation of an easy, graceful style of composition, and of much useful knowledge. Finally, at sixteen, his father gave him the choice of three things—to go to college, be a merchant, or work on the farm ; and he chose the last. In this employment, whether industrious or not, he acquired, by athletic labor and breathing the mountain air, that firm, enduring health and manly bearing to which he was indebted for such mental and physical energy so many years of his life.

The business of the store, however, had increased to such a degree that his father concluded to take him into it ; and it was a wise decision. There he began as other boys did, like a sailor before the mast, earning his promotion. He acquired habits of industry, method and punctuality. Under his excellent and judicious parent, he gained a knowledge of trade, he rose in trust, and at last was taken into partnership in the mercantile concern. He was also appointed Postmaster of Rindge. Soon after, in 1820, he married Miss Tryphosa Jewett, daughter of Dr. Stephen Jewett, of that place. She was the bride of his youth, on whom he used to look askance at church. She died on a visit to her native place, July 31, 1831, leaving four children, as named in the genealogy at the close of this memoir.

He had a taste for military tactics. Enrolled in the N. H. militia at sixteen, he made it an object of so much attention and pride, that he rose rapidly in office ; at twenty-one he was commissioned as Adjutant; at twenty-five, as Lieut. Colonel, and finally, at twenty-six, was chosen Colonel of the Regiment. He organized and equipped an independent company in his native town, of which he was chosen captain ; and among the New Hampshire mountain boys, there were few companies more popular than the Rindge Light Infantry.

As it is desirable to finish this department in the memoir of his life, it may be well to remark here, that after his removal to Boston he joined the Ancient and Honorable Artillery Company. There was a time in the history of this company, when the militia, so important as the guardian of peace, the protector of the laws and our *dernier resort* in time of trouble, had lost its influence, become degraded in popular favor, and was regarded by too many as a mere census of men and arms. Col. Wilder wished to see the militia restored to its pristine rank in public opinion, and did all in his power to promote a right military spirit for the defence of the country. This Company suffered, in common with others, but never lost sight of its antiquity and former high standing. Chartered in 1638, it has celebrated more than 200 anniversaries, on each of which, with few exceptions, some noted clergyman has delivered a sermon. Time has hallowed this patriotic festival ; and long, long has its return been a gala-day in the city and honored by the people. For twenty-five years Col. Wilder had never been absent from this celebration. In looking into its early history, it became still more endeared to its members ; for it is the only offspring in the world of the Royal Artillery Company of London, founded in 1537, and which by virtue of his rank the king commanded.

Col. Wilder, having been nominated four times and declined the honor, accepted the command in 1857. Induced to believe that his Royal Highness, Prince Albert, might be the commander of the parent company, he entered into a correspondence with him through our Minister, George M. Dallas, Esq., on the 1st of February, 1857, wherein he remarked: " Permit me also to state, that we regard the relation of these Companies as one of the many ties which bind young America to her old English Parent ; that we fondly cherish the hope, and the belief, that these bonds will never be sundered ; and we pray that peace and prosperity may crown both nations."

On receiving this letter, Lord Clarendon, on the 8th of April following, replied, enclosing a list of the present members of the Artillery Company of London, and a copy of the revised Rules and Regulations, and also at his Royal Highness's command a copy of Highmore's History of the Company to 1802, a scarce book ; and said, " His Royal Highness begs that the Company may be informed that he cannot but be highly gratified at the manner in which the Parent Company, of which he is at the head, is spoken of by its descendant at Boston; and he will be much obliged by your having the expression of his best thanks conveyed to Col. Wilder, for his kindness in sending his Royal Highness a copy of the History of the Boston Company, which he has looked over with much interest, and will have great pleasure in adding to his library."

At the 219th Anniversary of the Ancient and Honorable Artillery Company, June 1, 1857, the commander, " Col. Wilder, then put the question, as to whether his Royal Highness, Prince ALBERT, Field Marshal, Captain General, and Colonel of the Royal Artillery Company of London, should be made a Special Honorary Member of the Corps—an overwhelming shout of 'aye, aye,' was the response, accompanied with great applause." It was voted, on motion of Gen. Tyler, that the commander should inform Prince Albert of his election. In conclusion, Col. Wilder observed :

" Gentlemen—I must not trespass longer upon your time. The moment has arrived when we should call into action the big guns. But before I close, permit me to say that I accepted the command of this Company from a conviction that the existence of military power is the surest safeguard of civil authority, and from a desire to aid in perpetuating the history and fame of our Ancient Corps. For more than two centuries it has stood a faithful sentinel on the watch-tower of freedom. There may it stand forever !" [Prolonged heering.]

At the age of twenty-one, he commenced business under the firm of S. L. Wilder & Son. This continued till 1825, when he sought a wider field and moved to Boston. His acquaintance with military men and merchants in New Hampshire, gave him at once an extensive trade. In the wholesale W. I. goods business, under the firm of Wilder

& Payson, he began in Union Street: he pursued it under the firm of Wilder & Smith, North Market street; and then, in his own name, at No. 3 Central Wharf, was in the wholesale and importing line till 1837. He then became a partner in the Commission House of Parker, Blanchard & Wilder, Water street; afterwards, Parker, Wilder & Parker, Pearl street; and at the present time, Parker, Wilder & Co., Winthrop square, in a warehouse which is one of the most capacious and elegant structures in the city. This firm has also a branch in New York. Mr. Wilder has passed through various crises of commercial embarrassment, yet he has never failed to meet his obligations and maintain a fair and honorable reputation, and has been successful in business.

As a merchant his character stood high. He was sought for to fill stations of responsibility and trust. He was an original director in the Hamilton Bank and National Insurance Company, and has held those offices for more than thirty years; he has been a director for twenty years in the Mutual Life Insurance Company, and also in other institutions of the kind. The Merchants' Magazine for January, 1855, No. 187, contains a portrait and well drawn sketch of the principal events of his life to that date, and the description of his indefatigable perseverance, his urbanity as a gentleman, and his appearance at the desk of his counting-room, surrounded by files and masses of letters from numerous correspondents, is there faithfully portrayed.

But trade and wealth were not the all-engrossing pursuits of his mind; though too often the sole objects of those, who, absorbed in the details of commerce, become men of one idea—their horizon bounded by the money market—their delight in laying up for themselves treasures upon earth—until, with care-worn looks and anxious greed for more and more, they die, "passing through nature to eternity." Far from this was the philanthropic spirit of Mr. Wilder. In his prosperity he saw a wide field opening before him in which he could do good to others and benefit his country. He devoted a suitable time to business, and all his leisure to horticultural and agricultural pursuits. He spared no expense, he rested from no labors, to instil into the public mind a taste for such honorable and useful employments. He cultivated his grounds, imported trees, seeds and plants from distant countries, and thus by his example he endeavored to assist and elevate the rank of the husbandman.

Those who have resided long in Boston can well recollect the change which has taken place in our fruit market within a few years. They must have noticed with admiration the abundance of pears, apples, peaches, and strawberries of various kinds and delicious flavor, which in their season crowd the fruit stands ; flowers, too, of surpassing beauty and rareness bloom in our conservatories, ready to adorn the festival or soften the sorrows of the grave. Whence comes this astonishing improvement in the most salubrious as well as the most ornamental luxuries of life ? Go to the green-house, the suburban garden, or the large fruit-nursery, and inquire their history, and you will find they are the work of a few enterprising men, among whom the subject of this memoir stands in the foremost rank.

It has been already remarked, that in the year 1831 he was bereaved of her who was the " wife of his youth." She left four young children, and the home where he had been so happy was turned into gloom and darkness. He sought a change of residence, and finding a spot, which, from his love of rural life, was calculated to assuage his sorrow and loneliness by useful employment, he in 1832 purchased the country seat in Dorchester, originally built by Governor Increase Sumner, on the Roxbury line, and near Grove Hall ; here he has resided for thirty-five years. It is about three and a half miles from Boston. The house stands back from the road, on a lovely spot, in the midst of sylvan scenery. He has a handsome and choice library, to which he is no stranger—a large garden, orchard, greenhouses, and a forest of fruit trees. He seems early to have learned and practised, in all his pursuits, one of those grand principles which influence the whole course of life, the philosophy of habit—a power almost omnipotent for good or evil in human destiny. He is an early riser, and devotes the morning to study or writing, or in the season of cultivation to his men in the garden, directing their labors and often assisting them, and in the middle of the day attends to his mercantile affairs in the city. The evening is spent with his family and his books. Every thing is done by method and system. Numerous letters from abroad are received and answered. Thus passed several years while he was acquiring that knowledge and skill in the raising of fruits and flowers, which prepared him for the usefulness and honor which he attained. He could now speak from experience. He has in his

3

collection of the numerous plants and trees, 2500 pear trees, and has had more than 800 varieties of this fruit in his grounds. But, there is something so peculiar in the love and pursuit of knowledge, that it cannot rest alone, shut up and watched like the treasures of a miser; we long to impart it to others, and spread its blessings among them. Possessing this disposition, we find him joining or forming societies, in which he soon took the lead. Of such, a brief account will now claim the attention of the reader.

A charter was granted, June 12, 1829, to Zebedee Cook, Jr., Robert L. Emmons, William Worthington, B. V. French, John B. Russell, J. R. Newell, Cheever Newhall, and Thomas G. Fessenden with their associates, as a Massachusetts Horticultural Society. Gen. Henry A. S. Dearborn was elected its first President; Col. Wilder soon after joined it; and although their names do not appear among the grantees of the charter, yet in its early operations they were among its efficient and most energetic supporters. It was a darling object of Gen. Dearborn—and he soon found a warm coadjutor in Col. Wilder—to make the institution a blessing to the public and an honor to its members. He spent years in laying out and embellishing the grounds of Mount Auburn Cemetery in Cambridge; and to him Forest Hills Cemetery in Roxbury owes its origin and much of the striking but not gloomy scenery which surrounds that home of the dead. The grateful proprietors have erected a handsome monument to the memory of this excellent man, whose honored friendship the writer of this article regards among the sweetest reminiscences of his earlier days.

Many men of note early belonged to the Massachusetts Horticultural Society: John Lowell, Elias Phinney, Henry Colman, Robert Manning, Samuel G. Perkins and Alexander H. Everett, and also Judge Story and Daniel Webster, *par nobile fratrum*. Alas! not one of them survives.

Soon after the Society was formed, Dr. Jacob Bigelow, who for many years had been seeking an opportunity to found a Cemetery out of the city for the burial of the dead, suggested the expediency of purchasing Mount Auburn for this object, and also for an Experimental Garden. He presented a plan to the Society, and Gen. Dearborn, the President, was instructed to visit and examine the spot, and report on its adaptation.

The result was favorable. The premises, under the name of "Sweet Auburn," were owned by George W. Brimmer, Esq., who had commenced laying out and embellishing the grounds for his private residence ; but on solicitation he consented to dispose of them for $6000. On the report of Gen. Dearborn, resolutions were passed authorizing a purchase, provided a hundred gentlemen could be found to take burial lots at sixty dollars each ; which was done, Mr. Wilder being one of the number, and a conveyance was made ; and thus Mount Auburn was originally established as a Cemetery and Experimental Garden. "But the proprietors of these lots were not de facto members of the Horticultural Association, and in 1835 expressed a desire for a separation of the Cemetery from the Society. On Mr. Wilder's motion, a committee representing each of these interests was appointed, to mature a plan and agree on the conditions of separation. This body, of which Judge Story was chairman, acting for the proprietors of the cemetery, as Mr. Wilder and his associate, Hon. Elijah Vose, did for the members of the Horticultural Society, made many unsuccessful attempts at agreement, till the Judge, despairing of a union, arose and left the room. This was a critical moment for both institutions. Mr. W. saw the danger, and following the Judge, besought him to return, at the same time pledging him the most cordial co-operation in a new proposition for a settlement. They returned, and having resumed their seats, the subject of this sketch submitted a resolution, providing that one fourth part of the gross proceeds from the annual sale of lots, after deducting certain expenses, should be paid year by year by the proprietors to the Massachusetts Horticultural Society, in consideration of its relinquishing its right and title to the same."* This resolution prevailed, and became the basis of the separation of these two interests—a transaction in the highest degree beneficial to both—enabling the proprietors of Mount Auburn Cemetery to prosecute their world-renowned object with more singleness of purpose, and with greater success ; and also placing at the disposal of the Horticultural Society a considerable portion of the funds for the erection of a Hall in School street, and since for the elegant Temple in Tremont street. This in-

---

* "Portraits of Eminent Americans now living," by John Livingston, 1854.

come is both annual and perpetual, and the present year amounts to more than eight thousand dollars.

In 1840, Mr. Wilder was chosen the fourth President of the Society—an office to which he was annually elected for eight years. His first effort was to erect a Horticultural Hall. Being chairman of the building committee, which could not agree on a site, he and Josiah Stickney, Esq. purchased on private account the old Latin school-house in School street, and offered it to the Society, which was accepted. Mr. Wilder was requested, on the 14th day of September, 1841, to lay the corner stone; and on that day, in presence of the members and a large assembly of spectators, the ceremony was performed. In his address he observes:

" I cannot conclude my remarks without alluding to an act which should never be forgotten, a meritorious one—and be it ever remembered, that to this Society the community are indebted for the foundation and consecration of Mount Auburn Cemetery—that hallowed resting place for the dead—that ' Garden of Graves.' Noble act! glorious deed ! a measure calculated to reflect honor on any institution, and I doubt not it will redound to the credit of this, and will be gratefully remembered while this corner stone endures, and when we and the members of this institution shall be quietly reposing in the ' Field of Peace,' or sleeping beneath the sods of the valley."

A fine granite structure, ornamental to the city, was soon erected. It contained a hall for exhibition, library, committee room, and every convenience for that time. It was dedicated in the presence of Hon. John Quincy Adams, Gov. Briggs, and other distinguished gentlemen; and an ornate and appropriate address was delivered by the Hon. George Lunt. But in a few years this Hall proved insufficient. The increasing interest and enterprise of the Society demanded a still more commodious edifice, especially for the splendid contributions of fruits and flowers. An offer of $70,000 for the estate having been made by Mr. H. D. Parker—which was much more than the cost—they sold it to him, and he built on the spot an elegant addition to the Parker House, with its marble façade. On removal of the building, in 1857, the box containing the plate, documents, coins and memorials was opened, by order of the Society, by Mr. Wilder in presence of the members, the plate not being in the least tarnished, though sixteen years had elapsed. It was resealed, and deposited with the new box of memorials and documents, when the corner stone of the present superb Hall was laid in 1865.

The erection of the first Horticultural Hall and the exhibitions attracted public attention more and more ; and these were occasionally closed by a grand festival, in which ladies and gentlemen participated.

The Triennial Celebration of the Horticultural Society on Friday, the 19th day of September, 1845, at Faneuil Hall, was a brilliant and imposing spectacle ; whether we consider the assemblage of beauty—the array of intellectual power—or the display of fruits and flowers, in almost endless variety, which ornamented the tables, as though Flora and Pomona had met within the walls of this hallowed temple, and breathed a celestial aroma on the place. This joyous banquet commemorated their 17th anniversary.

Faneuil Hall had been fitted up with great taste, and was superbly decorated with wreaths and evergreens, roses and festoons of flowers. The panels of the galleries were filled on one side with the names of Lowell, Buel, Fessenden, Prince, Manning and Michaux :—on the other side with Loudon, Van Mons, Knight, Jussieu, Duhamel and Douglass, and in front those of Linnæus and De Candolle. Thirteen tables were spread with viands, fruits and bouquets—luxuries from abroad or the rich growth of suburban gardens. Surrounding these appeared six hundred ladies and gentlemen, and on the platform, with a seat a little raised for the President, sat Daniel Webster, the venerable Josiah Quincy, Robert C. Winthrop, Caleb Cushing, Geo. S. Hillard, and delegates from other States ; and there was the Rev. Dr. John Codman, the pastor of Col. Wilder, who invoked the blessing. Over all this festal scene the portrait of the immortal WASHINGTON hung from the walls, stirring up the memory of his glory and love of rural life. And, as though it needed one more eminent Bostonian there to make the festival complete in all its parts, suddenly a Committee at the door announced the arrival of a guest, who on reaching the platform was introduced by the President in this happy manner :—

"Ladies and Gentlemen: It is with feelings of high gratification that I am enabled to present to you a distinguished member of our association, who after an absence of several years of honorable service at the Court of St. James, has this day arrived on the shores of New England. I introduce to your cordial greeting, his Excellency EDWARD EVERETT." [Great applause.]

Many excellent sentiments, accompanied with music and original songs, enlivened the occasion, but they must be passed over and only a few extracts offered from the eloquent speeches which crowned the banquet. The President commenced with a few appropriate remarks on the institution, and observed—

" Sixteen years ago this day, its first exhibition was held in the Exchange Coffee House in this city, and as an illustration of the great success and prosperity that has attended the efforts of its members, I quote from the published Report of the Society. The number of the contributors on that occasion was thirty-two ; the baskets and dishes of fruits less than one hundred ; and the amount of premiums offered, less than $200. And as a further illustration, I notice by this Report that the contribution of Robert Manning, the Pomologist of America, consisted of but one basket of peaches ; while at the present exhibition, the family of that lamented man have sent us 240 varieties of the pear. And in a note I received from him a short time previous to his decease, he stated that he had gathered into his own collection, from a point of time but a few years antecedent to the formation of the institution, nearly 2,000 varieties of fruits." . . .

" I congratulate the Society on the liberal and increasing patronage of the community—on the addition of more than 100 new members to its ranks, during the last nine months—on the continued improvement in the productions exhibited—on the honorable and elevated standing our institution sustains both at home and abroad—and on the harmony and union that prevail among us." . . . .

The President then proposed—

" *Our late Minister to the Court of St. James.* We honor him as a scholar, we respect him as a statesman, and we love him as a noble specimen of the fruits of New England culture." [Loud cheers.]

Mr. Everett—

" I am greatly indebted to you for this cordial reception. I cannot but feel under great obligations to the Massachusetts Horticultural Society, of which I have long had the honor of being a member—though a very unprofitable one—that the first voice of salutation which reached me on returning home, proceeded from them. Our respected fellow-citizens, Messrs. Josiah Bradlee and Stephen Fairbanks, on their morning stroll through East Boston, were good enough, before I had set foot on *terra firma*, to convey to me your kind invitation. . . . . . . I regret that I am so little able to thank you in a proper manner. I have been so lately rocking upon the Atlantic, whose lullaby is not always the gentlest, that I am hardly fit for rocking in the ' Old Cradle of Liberty,' to which your kind note of this morning invited me. I almost unconsciously catch at the table to steady myself, expecting that the flowers and fruits will fetch away in some lee-lurch ; and even the pillars of Old Faneuil Hall, not often found out of the true plumb-line, seem to reel over my head. . . .

" The shores of Newfoundland and Nova Scotia, as we coasted along them, seemed to have a claim upon us, as a part of our native continent, and made us feel that we had at length crossed the world-dividing deep :—and when about sunrise this morning, after stretching down from Halifax, against a stiff south-wester, I beheld Cape Ann light-house at a dim and misty distance, I must say that I thought it one of the most beautiful pieces of architecture I ever beheld. I do not know to what particular order it belongs, nor the proportion of the height to the diameter. And as to the ornaments of the capital, Mr. President, whether they are acanthus or lotus, or any other flower in your conservatory, I am quite unable to say :—but this I will say, that after seeing many of the finest buildings in the old world and the new, I came to the conclusion, at about six o'clock this morning, that Cape Ann Light-house beats them all." [Applause.] . . .

The President then gave—

" *The Marshfield Farmer.* ' All head in counsel, all wisdom in speech : '—always ready to defend the soil and to make the soil more and more worth defending."

To which Mr. Webster responded—

" Ladies and Gentlemen: There are far better farmers in Marshfield than I am, but as I see none of them present, I suppose that I am bound to take the compliment to myself. . . . Mr. President, as it has been said from the chair, and in the sentiments round the table, it is our fortune in New England to live beneath a somewhat rugged sky, and till a somewhat hard and unyielding earth; but something of hardness, of unfavorable condition and circumstances, seems necessary to excite human genius, labor and skill, and bring forth the results most useful and honorable to man. I greatly doubt whether all the luxuriance of the tropics, and all that grows under the fervid sky of the equator, can equal the exhibition of flowers made to-day amid these northern latitudes. Here, there is all the brilliancy of color and all the gorgeous display of tropical regions; but there, the display is made in swamps and jungles abounding in noxious reptiles; it is not the result of cultivation, taste and human labor working on the capacity of Nature. Sir, I congratulate you that our flowers are not

> ' Born to blush unseen
> And waste their sweetness on the desert air.'

The botany we cultivate, the productions of the business of horticulture, the plants of the garden, are cultivated with us, by hands as delicate as their own tendrils, viewed by countenances as spotless and pure as their own petals, and watched by eyes as brilliant and full of lustre as their own beautiful exhibitions of splendor. [Applause.] . . . . . Mr. President, we who belong to the class of farmers are compelled to bring nothing but our applause to those whose taste, condition and position enable them to contribute these horticultural excellences which we see around us. But the honor belongs to the State, and I shall not trespass beyond the bounds of reason and justice, if I say that there could nowhere, *nowhere* be a more perfect and tasteful exhibition of horticultural products than we have witnessed in this city the present week. Let this good work speed. May this good work go prospering and to prosper. And as we live in a country which produces a race of hard working men, and the most useful fruits of the earth, so let us show every year that it is not less productive of beautiful flowers—as it certainly is not of graceful hands to entwine them." [Applause.] . . . .

He was followed by the Hon. Josiah Quincy, late President of Harvard University, and by the Hon. Robert C. Winthrop, in appropriate remarks, which the want of space forbids us to insert.

To the toast given by the President—

" *The Central Flowery Nation of China.* We welcome the man who has united by closer ties the gardens of the East and the gardens of the West, our late Minister to the Celestial Empire—"

The Hon. Caleb Cushing replied, in a few eloquent remarks:

. . " Here alone—here, and in Christian lands, woman enchants and beautifies with her presence the festive scene. Woman, our equal—shall I not say our moral superior. It is only here that such a scene can gladden the human eye. I regard this exhibition as a striking proof of the point which education and intellectual refinement have reached in our country, that we have got beyond mere utility, and ceasing to inquire how far it is incompatible with beauty, have found that the beautiful is itself useful. We have learned to admire art—to appreciate painting and sculpture—and to look upon fruits and flowers as models of delicacy and beauty. And although it is said that Massachusetts produces nothing but the ice of her lakes and the granite of her hills, yet we know that she also produces men, freehearted, high-minded, noble-purposed men and women—the fairest and best. They are also the most beautiful growth of the land. It is here that we have the best proof of the intellectual and moral elevation to which our favored State has ascended."

To a toast, " *The Boston Orators,*" Mr. Hillard responded in his usually elegant style :

. . . "Your triumphs and successes are recorded upon a page wide as the living land-scape, and bounded by no margin less than the horizon. Every tree which waves in the wind is vocal with your good works, and every flower that holds up its painted cup to drink the dew of the morning seems redolent with your praise."

And he concluded with offering the following sentiment—

" *The Gardens of our Country.* May the apple of discord never grow there, nor the ser-pent of disunion glide among their bowers."

The Third Triennial Celebration of the Horticultural Society was held at Faneuil Hall, Sept. 22, 1848. It was embellished in a similar style as the other festivals. Upon the supporting columns of an arch, were the names of Dearborn, Cook, Vose and Wilder, Presidents of the Society, on one side ; and on the other, those of Appleton, Brad-lee, Lowell, and Lyman, benefactors. A large assemblage of ladies and gentlemen were at the banquet. Among the guests on the platform, on the right of the President, sat Madam Alexander Hamilton, and around were the Clergy, Robert C. Winthrop, Speaker of the H. of Representatives in Congress, Josiah Quincy, Jr., Mayor of Boston, Ex-Gov. Seward of New York, the venerable Josiah Quincy, Ex-Pres. of Harvard University, Gen. H. A. S. Dearborn, John S. Skinner of Philadelphia, A. J. Downing of New York, Morton McMichael, Chairman of Delegation from the Pennsylvania Society, Hon. James Arnold, President of the New Bedford Society, Dr. Thompson of the Delaware Society, and delegates from many kindred associations. Rev. Wm. M. Rogers asked the blessing.

Sentiments and speeches followed the dinner. An extract is of-fered from the parting Address of the President, as he tendered his resignation ; and, as one of the sentiments reminds us, it was on his fiftieth birth-day. Mr. Wilder said—

" But the time has arrived when in my own judgment it is proper that I should signify my intention to take official leave—and this I now do. If honor has attached to the office, I have surely had it lavished on me—if labor and anxiety, then I humbly claim to have borne my share ; but wherever I live or wherever I may go, the name of the Massachusetts Horticultural Society will cause a thrill of joy and pleasure, until this heart shall cease to beat ; and should I be so fortunate as to retain in your hearts an affectionate remembrance, it will be my highest honor, my richest reward.

" One of the best pieces of advice that great writer, Sir Walter Scott, ever gave was to plant a *tree.* ' When you have time,' said he, ' *plant a tree,* it will be growing when you are sleeping.' Yes, ladies and gentlemen, when we are sleeping in the dust, and generations shall rise up and bless us for the deed, and

' Our children's children shall enjoy the fruit.'

And as an inheritance in my family, after that of a good moral and religious education, one of the greatest blessings which I desire to leave for them, is a garden well stocked with fruit and flowers; and when they are partaking of these luxuries of God's bounty, will they not shed a tear of gratitude and remember the hand that planted it?

"The time will not permit extended remarks—one word, however, as to the future prospects of our Society. They are of the most cheering character. Within the last five years its list of members has been more than doubled; its new Hall, in School street, erected and furnished; its funds considerably augmented, and although its expenditures are on a arge and liberal scale, yet it is believed that with its income from Mount Auburn, the day is not distant when its sinking fund will extinguish the debt, and leave means commensurate for all reasonable wants.

"For eight years I have annually been elected as its President, and since my first election, with but two dissenting votes—a unanimity far beyond my merit, and for which, and the cordial and vigorous support I have received from my official associates, I desire now and ever to cherish the most profound thankfulness and gratitude."

Mr. Webster then arose and said, "Ladies and Gentlemen, I have obtained leave of the President to remind this company that a venerable lady honors this occasion with her presence. She is the daughter of Gen. Philip Schuyler, of the Revolutionary army, and the widow of Alexander Hamilton." [Great cheering.]

To this the President responded in behalf of Madam Hamilton.

He then announced this sentiment—alluding to Faneuil Hall Market and the Cochituate water:

"*The City of Boston.* Among her varieties of fruits, she has two Quincy's (Quinces) which she intends to preserve—one in 'granite' the other in 'pure water.'"

In reply to this, his Honor Josiah Quincy, Jr., rose; but for the eloquent remarks of himself and other distinguished men, I am compelled to refer to the Report of the "Twentieth Annual Exhibition of the M. H. Society," September, 1848. The sentiments were full of wit, and the speeches of a high order. They will fully reward the reader of that pamphlet. One short paragraph must suffice. Gen. Dearborn, first President of the Society, observed, "When, riding through our highways, I see one shrub by the door or flower pot in the window, I consider it the emblem of virtue and refinement, of all that is good and commendable in man or woman, and I say to myself 'That is a good family, well managed, well educated, and in the right way to respect and confidence.'"

When the President retired, Vice President French, after a just compliment to his talents, skill and fidelity, offered this sentiment:

"*The President of the Massachusetts Horticultural Society.* May the remainder of his life be as prosperous and happy, as his former years have been brilliant and useful to his country."

4

With the close of this year, Mr. Wilder's administration as President terminated—long to be remembered as a successful and brilliant period in the history of the Society. Votes of thanks were passed by them, as a testimonial of their gratitude for his labors and services, accompanied with complimentary resolutions, and a superb silver pitcher, of the value of one hundred and fifty dollars.

That the partiality of friends has not exaggerated nor the lapse of nearly twenty years depreciated the importance of his services, will appear by the following extracts from the Address of Charles M. Hovey, Esq., President of the Society, at laying the corner-stone of the Hall in Tremont street, September 3, 1864:

"But it is since the completion of the former Hall, that the progress of the Society has been more rapid, and its influence felt throughout the country. New life and fresh vitality were infused into the Society. It had the sympathy as it had the substantial aid of the public. It was appreciated as its founders intended it should be. Its objects seemed all at once to become apparent."

Also at the Dedication of the same, September, 1865:

"Fortunate was the Society in having in its presiding officer one who was so thoroughly imbued with the love of Horticulture, whose leisure hours were devoted to its pursuits, whose means enabled him to introduce various new fruits, plants and flowers, and whose distinguished services in Pomology continue up to this day, though now lessened by illness; but whose presence we hail to-day with more than ordinary pleasure after an absence of nearly two years."

Floriculture was not neglected while he held this office. His Camellia house was supposed to have contained the best collection in the country at that time, and would compare favorably with any thing of the kind abroad. Of the history of this plant he furnished an article in Hovey's Magazine of Horticulture, Vol. i. p. 13, "Observations on the Camellia, with some account of its introduction into Great Britain and this country." He had many hundred varieties of this elegant tribe, with thousands of plants and seedlings secured by Hybridization, of which he gave a scientific account in the Proceedings of the Massachusetts Horticultural Society, Vol. i. p. 35, "The Hybridization of the Camellia and its varieties." In honor of the producer, the Society named one of these plants Camellia Wilderii, the other Mrs. Abby Wilder, and awarded him a premium of fifty dollars. Colored plates of them handsomely executed may be seen in the Illustrated volumes of the above periodical. The stock of these two varieties he disposed of to Mr. Warren for $1000, who afterwards sold some of the plants at a high price in this country and in Europe. Other seedlings have been dedicated to members of his family.

But it was in Pomology that Mr. Wilder greatly excelled, and was so widely known. He had imported fruit trees from England, France, Belgium and Germany. His correspondence at home and abroad was extensive. No pains, no expense was spared to disseminate trees and grafts of the best kinds of fruit. Mr. Livingston justly remarks, " In his orchards the pear occupies a place corresponding with that of the Camellia in his green-houses." More than three hundred varieties of the pear have been brought from his grounds to a single exhibition, and for several years he took the first premium of the Massachusetts Horticultural Society for the best collection. The peculiar manner in which he preserved them until spring he communicated by request to the Agricultural Society, in 1852, and published an account of it in the New England Farmer, Vol. iv. p. 103.

After his resignation of the presidency of the Massachusetts Horticultural Society, he headed a circular in which several kindred institutions joined, for a convention of fruit growers, with the object of promoting and disseminating knowledge of pomology throughout the country ; and on the 10th of October, 1848, a large meeting, composed of influential gentlemen from various States, was held, under the auspices of the American Institute, New York. They organized, unanimously chose Mr. Wilder their President, and adopted the name of the " National Congress of Fruit Growers."

But, the march of improvement is not always smooth ; a cloud will sometimes rise in the most auspicious sky. " Without opposition," says Mr. Livingston, " another meeting of pomologists was held in connection with the New York State Agricultural Society's annual exhibition, and was organized as the ' National Pomological Convention.' " This was a damper. Two societies of a similar kind could not co-operate so successfully, or bring such power and influence to bear on this important object, as the united efforts of one grand association. They therefore chose a joint committee of conference, of which Mr. Wilder was chairman, and the result was a consolidation under the name of the American Pomological Congress, since altered to the American Pomological Society. They agreed on biennial celebrations—one at Cincinnati in the autumn of 1850, the next at Philadelphia in 1852. From that time the union has been cordial, and greatly beneficial to the public. Mr. Wilder, being detained by domestic affliction, was not present at Cincinnati, and Dr. W. D. Brinckle, of Philadelphia, was elected to the chair; but at the next meeting he resigned the office and Mr. Wilder was re-elected.

An event, however, had occurred shortly before this, which cast a gloom over all hearts devoted to rural taste and science. Andrew Jackson Downing, of Newburg, New York, for whom Mr. Wilder had long cherished a warm friendship, and who had co-operated with him in the formation of this Society, perished in the Henry Clay, when that steamer was burnt on the Hudson River, July 28, 1852. The loss of such a man was a heavy blow to the whole community. His publications and labors had a world-wide reputation. He wrote that popular work, "Fruits and Fruit Trees of America," dedicated to Mr. Wilder, who was requested by the Horticultural Societies of Massachusetts and Pennsylvania, to prepare his Eulogy for the approaching convention at Philadelphia, in September. It was one of his happiest productions, worthy of the friend whose loss he deplored. A few extracts are all our limited space will allow:

"But Downing has gone! His seat in this Congress is vacant; another will make the report which was expected from him. We shall much miss his wise and leading counsels in our deliberations and discussions, his prompt and energetic action in our endeavors to advance the worthy objects of this association, in the origin and progress of which his energy was so conspicuous. He has gone! He is numbered with those patrons and promoters of the ornamental and useful arts who rest from their labors—with the erudite and sage Pickering, the wise and laborious Buel, the ardent and scientific Mease, the humorous and poetic Fessenden, the practical and enterprising Lowell, the tasteful and enthusiastic Dearborn, the indefatigable and versatile Skinner, the scientific Loudon, and others of noble designs and enduring fame. These have fallen around us like the leaves of autumn; and Providence now calls us to inscribe on that star-spangled roll the cherished name of DOWN-ING, struck down suddenly, when his sun was at the zenith of his glory.

"He rests in the bosom of his mother earth, in the city of his birth and in the sepulchre of his fathers, on the banks of that beautiful river, where his boyhood sported, and where the choicest scenery inspired his opening mind with the love of nature—a spot which will be dear to the thousands of his admirers, and which our love to him will constrain us to visit. We may resort to his hospitable mansion; but he will no longer greet us with his cordial salutation, nor extend to us the right hand of fellowship. We may wend our way through his beautiful grounds; but he will not be there to accompany us. Instead of his pleasant and instructive voice, which once dropped words of wisdom and delight on our ear, we shall hear the trees mournfully sighing in the breezes—the cypress moaning his funeral dirge, and the willow weeping in responsive grief 'because he is not.' 'His mortal has put on immortality.'

"When we think of the place which he occupied in the hearts of his countrymen and contemporaries—the expanding interest which he has awakened in the rural arts, the refinements and comforts of society—of his plans, which others, inspired by his genius, will unfold and consummate—and of his works which will be admired when the tongues that now praise him shall be silent in death, our sense of justice accords to him an earthly immortality—a fame which history will cherish, art adorn, and grateful posterity revere." *

The next session of the American Pomological Society was in Boston, Sept. 13, 1854, which was enlivened by a Levee at the Revere House, given by Mr. Wilder to the members on the occasion. It met at Rochester, N. Y., in September, 1856; in the city of New York in 1858; at Philadelphia in 1860; in Boston in 1862; at Rochester, N. Y. in 1864; and was to meet at St. Louis, Mo., 1866, but from the prevalence of the cholera there, the meeting was postponed to the present year, 1867, Mr. Wilder continuing as President. The following paragraphs have been selected from his Addresses at some of these meetings.

At Rochester, 1856.

After discoursing on the disappointments and obstacles incident to the cultivation of fruit, he observes:

"Let nothing discourage you in this hopeful department of pomology. Go on, persevere;

'Give new endeavors to the mystic art,
Try every scheme, and riper views impart;
Who knows what meed thy labors may await?
What glorious fruits thy conquest may create?'

"These are triumphs worthy of the highest ambition, conquests which leave no wound on the heart of memory, no stain on the wing of time. He, who only adds one really valuable variety to our list of fruits, is a public benefactor. I had rather be the man who planted that umbrageous tree, from whose bending branches future generations shall pluck the luscious fruit, when I am sleeping beneath the clods of the valley, than he who has conquered armies. I would prefer the honor of introducing the Baldwin apple, the Seckel pear, Hovey's Seedling strawberry, aye, or the Black Tartarian cherry from the Crimea, to the proudest victory which has been won upon that blood-stained soil.

"Let us endeavor to disseminate the knowledge of the few among the many, that we may improve the public taste, add to the wealth of our republic, and confer on our countrymen the blessings of our favorite art. Thus shall we make other men happy, and keep them so—render our own homes the abodes of comfort and contentment, and hasten the time when the garden shall feel no blight, the fruitful field laugh with abundance, and rivers of gladness water the earth."

* Mr. Downing was a friend to whom Mr. Wilder was much attached. There was a similarity of pursuits and a congeniality of tastes in their lives. And what lover of Nature can ever look upon the cozy cottage with its little garden, the elegant villa, and the beautiful landscape scenery in our suburban improvements, without realizing how much we owe to the genius of Downing—a man who delighted to make others happy even in the humblest condition of humanity.

The loss of such a man brings to mind the elegiac ode of Horace, when lamenting the death of Quintilius, so dear to Virgil:

Multis ille bonis flebilis occidit,
Nulli flebilior quam tibi Virgili.

Though many a good man mourned the dead,
No tears like thine for him were shed.

NEW YORK, 1858.

In speaking of the enjoyments of such a pursuit and its influences, he says:

"And how delightful is the employment of the pomologist, going forth among his well-trained trees:

'To visit how they prosper, bud and bloom.'

His love is always young and fresh, ever approaching them with keener relish and increased affection. They, in return, recompensing every kind attention, 'clap their hands for joy,' and like those flowers of Paradise touched by the fair hand of Eve, *more gladly grow.*

"The more I investigate the laws of vegetable physiology, the more I am filled with wonder and reverence at the benevolent provisions of nature—at the instructive lessons which she teaches. Our trees—from the opening bud to the golden harvest—from the laying off of their gay autumnal livery, and during their rest in winter's shroud, waiting a resurrection to a new and superior life, are all eloquent preachers, proclaiming to our inmost soul—

'The hand that made us is Divine.'

"Taught by their counsels, who does not admire the wisdom, perfection and beauty of this fair creation! *The tiny bud,* encased in coats of mail so that the rude blasts may not visit it too roughly, rivalling in its mechanism the human eye, and destined to perpetuate its own species distinctive as the soul of man!——*the enamelled blossom,* unfolding her virgin bosom to the warm embrace of vernal air, bespangling the orchard with starry spray scarcely less beautiful than the glittering host above, dancing in rainbow hues, and flinging on the breeze a fragrance richer than the spices of Ceylon's Isles; sweet harbinger of bountiful harvest!——*the luscious fruits,* God's best gift to man, save woman—the melting *pear,* rough or polished rind, with sweetest honied flavor—the burnished *apple,* tempting human taste from the mother of our race to her last fair daughter—the royal *grape,* clustering beneath its bower of green, making glad the heart of man—the brilliant *cherry,* suffused with loveliest tints of rose and white or dyed in deepest incarnadine—the velvet *peach,* mantled with beauty's softest blush and vieing with the oriency of the morning—the delicious *plum,* veiled with silvery bloom, over robes of azure, purple, or cloth of vegetable gold! But what imagination can conceive, what pencil sketch, the changing hues, the varied magnificence and glory, when Pomona pours from her overflowing lap, the ripened treasures of the year! These, all these, are original designs, such as the genius of a Corregio, a Claude Lorraine, and the oldest masters could only imitate.

"Here, are creations, originally pronounced *very good.* Here, are inexhaustible sources of pleasure, beauties which fade only to appear again. Here, 'life flows pure, the heart more calmly beats.' Here, like the foliage and fruit falling from trees of favorite care, the true pomologist, after a well spent day, lies down to rest in the hope of a fairer to-morrow—in the glorious hope of partaking of the fruit of that tree, which 'yieldeth its fruit every month, and whose leaves are for the healing of the nations.'"

IN BOSTON, 1862.

"The more, therefore, we instil into the minds of our youth the love of our delightful art, the more will they appreciate the wisdom, beauty, and perfection of the external world, and the more will their souls become invested with that purity and refinement which enlarge the sphere of social happiness, and elevate the mind to contemplate with reverence and delight that Infinite Source,

'Which sends Nature forth the daughter of the skies,
To dwell on earth and charm all human eyes.'

"And when our work on earth is finished, how precious the monuments which this art rears to perpetuate our memories! It was the custom of some of the ancients to bury their dead under trees, so that future generations might sit over their graves screened from the parching heat, and dedicate fruits and flowers to distinguished men.

"What honorable testimonial to have a luscious fruit dedicated to your, memory—a fruit which shall bear the name not only of yourself, but of your family long after you shall have been buried beneath the sods of the valley! How transporting the thought, that future generations will sit under the cooling shade of the tree reared by your own hand, and regale themselves with its precious fruit! How chastening the anticipation, that when we shall have been gathered to our fathers, and these frail tenements are consigned to the bosom of our mother earth, the particles of our bodies shall be regenerated and reappear in the more beautiful forms of fruit or flower, and shall thus minister to the comfort of generations to come. Oh! let me be remembered in some graceful tree, some beautiful flower, some luscious fruit. Oh! yes, far better than storied monument or sculptured urn, let me be remembered as one who labored to adorn and improve the earth, to promote the pleasure and welfare of those who are to follow me."

Though in all his previous addresses he had confined himself to the objects and pursuits of the Society, yet on this occasion he could not overlook the unhappy condition of our country, and utters the following patriotic sentiments :

"At a crisis so momentous and fearful, involving our existence as an independent and united people, and our relation to every other nation under heaven, our paramount duty is plain. We must support with all our means that good Government which the patriotism and wisdom of our fathers established, and which, after every effort to avert the evil, is compelled to robe even her white-winged messenger of peace in the fiery habiliaments of war for the preservation of the Republic and the enforcement of its laws. We must hold on to the Constitution as the very palladium of our liberties, and the sheet anchor of our hope.

"The cloud, that overshadows us, is indeed dark and foreboding, yet we trust it will retire gilded with the bow of promise, and radiant with a hope of a brighter to-morrow. We believe that He who rules in mercy as well as in justice, will in the end bring our beloved nation out of all its troubles, and make us a wiser and a better people. Terrible as this crisis is, we doubt not that the progress of this great Republic is to be onward and upward in the cause of freedom, civilization and humanity, and in all that tends to the development of the comfort, happiness and perfection of the human race. Yes, we fondly cling to the hope that the day is coming yet, when war shall wash his bloody hand and sheathe his glittering sword—when our fields shall no longer be ploughed with the deadly cannon, or fertilized with the blood of our brethren—and when peace shall again wreathe her olive leaves around these distracted States, and bind them together in harmony and fraternal love. The night is dark, but the morning cometh. That golden age is ' coming yet.'

'Its coming yet for a' that,
When man to man the warld o'er,
Shall brothers be for a' that.'"

Mr. Wilder has just ordered the next meeting of this Society to be held at St. Louis, Mo., Sept. 11, 1867.

But we must now call the attention of the reader to his labors for the promotion of Agriculture. Soon after he had closed his administration as President of the Horticultural Society, he was solicited to join in a call for the establishment of an Agricultural Society in his own county. In pursuance thereof, a Convention was held at Dedham, Feb. 7, 1849. The Hon. Charles Francis Adams, now our

Minister to England, presided as chairman. The Norfolk Agricultural Society was organized; a constitution was reported by a committee, of which Mr. Wilder was chairman, and being accepted, he was chosen President and Mr. Adams Vice President. The sum of $3000 was subscribed for a fund, and the Society incorporated March 27, 1849.

The first Annual Cattle Show of this Society was held at Dedham, Sept. 26, 1849, a fair day and one long to be remembered. There were said to have been present ten thousand persons on that occasion. An Address was delivered by the President, in which the history of agriculture, its importance, its benefit to the community and means of advancement were prominent features. The Society appreciating its value, voted that three thousand copies be printed.

The banquet was remarkable—not merely a festival, but an intellectual feast. There for the first time ladies at the agricultural entertainment graced the table. Many of our first citizens were present: Gov. Briggs, Lieut. Gov. Read, Daniel Webster, Edward Everett, Robert C. Winthrop, Ex-Gov. Lincoln, Ex-Gov. Hill of New Hampshire, Charles Francis Adams, Josiah Quincy both father and son, Gen. Dearborn, Horace Mann, with many others of high respect. The voices too of song were not silent—they were heard in the Odes of the Rev. John Pierpont and the Hon. Tristam Burges.

Mr. Webster spoke eloquently of the influences of associations:

" We saw it years ago—perhaps I might say centuries ago. It began in the corporation of cities of the old world. It began in professional associations in the old world, in the legal, the medical and the theological. But it was long in that country and in this, before this principle of combination came to be acted upon in the great system of Agriculture."

It was here that Mr. Webster made his famous Turnip Speech, in which he remarked:

" It is just as certain as any thing in the world, it would be impossible for the cultivation of England to go on without the culture of turnips. . . . . I see that the turnip crop is the very soul and substance of English husbandry, I see that England would fail to pay the interest of her national debt if turnips were excluded from her culture." [Laughter and applause.]

Mr. Everett portrayed the happiness of the life of a farmer:

" I believe it to be the occupation most favorable to health, to tranquillity of mind, to simple manners, to frugal habits, to equality of condition. And what more do you want to make up an occupation most favorable to happiness? Certainly, there is no other pursuit, which to the same degree lies at the basis of the entire social system. I am not speaking without warrant, Mr. President, for you have told us the same thing in better language. Such is the consenting judgment of the world."

But the reader must be referred to the first volume of the Transactions of the Norfolk Agricultural Society for a further history. Yet there was one sentiment too rich to pass over and too true to be forgotten. It was offered by the Hon. Josiah Quincy, Jr. :

"*The Future Meetings of the Norfolk Agricultural Society.* They may have better cattle —they may have a more extended show ; but when will the breed of men—the native stock or the imported breed—equal that of their first meeting ?"

Alas ! nearly eighteen years have passed since this splendid festival, and how many of these bright stars have sunk below the horizon ! At a subsequent exhibition the President alluded to some of those who had departed. Of Gen. Dearborn he remarked :

"It affords me great pleasure to bear public testimony to the brilliant talents and great worth of our lamented Dearborn—a testimony which is the result of more than twenty years intimate acquaintance with him, in our favorite pursuits, and in official duty. His labors in the establishment of the Massachusetts Horticultural Society, the Mount Auburn and the Forest Hills Cemeteries, are proud and durable memorials of his skill, energy and taste. No enterprise was too bold for him to attempt ; no sacrifice was too great for him to make ; no labors too arduous for him to perform, in order to promote the intelligence, the refinement, virtue, welfare and renown of his countrymen."

The Norfolk Society was the first in the State to purchase grounds, build a Hall and take fees for admission. By the following extract from the address at the exhibition in 1854, the reader will see how the Society had prospered and what vigorous efforts they were making :

"Within the short period of five years, the Society has acquired funds to purchase the grounds on which its shows have heretofore been held ; has paid for the structures and other accommodations for the stock on exhibition ; and the present year has erected an agricultural hall, a building 130 feet in length, 55 in width and 28 in height. This edifice is pronounced by competent judges firm and durable ; it is of good architectural proportions and external finish, and contains on the lower floor an exhibition room and offices, and on the upper floor a spacious dining and audience hall, sufficient to accommodate at its tables one thousand persons."

In the year 1859 the Society purchased seven more acres of land, and thereby incurred a debt which, with subsequent improvements, amounted to about eight thousand five hundred dollars. To cancel it, efforts were made before the rebellion ; but in consequence of Mr. Wilder's sickness they were suspended. He assured the Society that the debt would and should be paid, if his life was spared. Within a year past this has been accomplished, principally by liberal subscribers.

From the organization of the Norfolk Society to this, now its eighteenth year, they have held their annual exhibitions. They have been successful and of increasing benefit to the community. Every year has had its Address, and every festival been enlivened by kindred spirits. Mr. Wilder has been annually re-elected as President, and still holds that office. A just appreciation of his services may be best understood by the following remarks from Gov. Bullock when he concluded his speech at the last annual celebration in Dedham, in 1866 :

" I meet here to-day, the members of this useful and prosperous Society of Norfolk, sitting and rejoicing under the presidency of one who has applied the results of well-earned commercial fortune to the development of the capacities of the earth, so largely and so liberally, that in every household and at every fireside in America, where the golden fruit of summer and autumn gladdens the sideboard or the hearth-stone, his name, his generosity, and his labors, are known and acknowledged."

In the year 1851, under a resolution of the Norfolk Agricultural Society, he proposed a Convention of the Agricultural Societies of the State.* This met at the State House ; and on their assembling he was

---

* Efforts had been made to obtain a Department of Agriculture as a branch of the government, and these having failed, Mr. W. explains the cause of failure, as will be seen in the following letter to Hon. Levi Lincoln :

Boston, May 15, 1851.

Hon. LEVI LINCOLN :

My Dear Sir,—I write to state what you have already learned by the papers, that the bill for the establishment of a State Board of Agriculture has been rejected in the House. The bill came up early last Monday morning, when two hundred members were absent, and unfortunately those upon whom we relied to advocate its claims. Two or three foolish speeches, filled (as I learn) with the old tirade against " book farming " and " scientific agriculture " were made, which gave the cast, there being no one to defend the bill, and all being desirous of clearing the Speaker's table before entering the Hoosac Tunnel. I have been absent from home a good deal of late, and therefore could not lobby with the members, a thing which by the bye I despise. I was assured, however, by those who promised to look after the matter, that it would be agreeable to all parties, and would pass without objection. In this we have been sadly outwitted and disappointed. That the principles of the bill are generally satisfactory to all those who believe in the advancement of art by aid of science, there can be no doubt ; and although you with others have zealously labored, midst discouragements and disappointments for a quarter of a century, to place this heaven-appointed profession on a par with the other arts and pursuits of life, I cannot doubt but your wishes are about to be realized. The indications from various parts of our country sanction this belief. The present condition of the agriculture of our country, and particularly of New England, call for the efforts of philanthropists to come forward in its aid. The results achieved by the application of science in Europe are truly astonishing in this branch of human industry. The crops of wheat which were but a few years since (in England and Scotland) only fifteen bushels per acre, have been raised in many instances to thirty-eight bushels, and a similar advance has taken place in other crops. . . . . . But I am not discouraged, nor disheartened. We have with us troops of ardent and devoted friends to the cause, and the day is not distant when our desires will in a measure be accomplished. Fortunately we have the " Central Board of Agriculture," about to be organized, and I trust the association will be of essential benefit to our various Societies, and the means of great good to all concerned. I have received certificates of the election of delegates from ten of the Societies, and now only await the return from your Society and one other, before we issue notice of the first meeting. May we hear from you on this point as early as your convenience will permit.

chosen Chairman. They then resolved themselves into a Central State Board of Agriculture, and elected him President.

It was voted, at the third session of this Agricultural Board, to memorialize the Legislature again in regard to an Agricultural Department of State, and Mr. Wilder, the Hon. Edward Everett, Prof. Wm. C. Fowler and others were appointed to draw and present the memorial. It was successful, and a State Board of Agriculture was established. Like that of the Board of Education, it has contributed much to the welfare and advancement of the community. He was appointed by the Governor, has been a member of this Board eleven years, and is now elected for three years more by the Norfolk Agricultural Society.

Nor should his influence and numerous addresses in behalf of an Agricultural College be forgotten. It was while he was President of the Senate of Massachusetts, that he submitted a Bill to this effect, which passed the Senate without a dissenting voice, but was lost in the House of Representatives. In consequence of this failure, he procured the passage of a resolve for the appointment of a board of five commissioners, of which he was Chairman, to examine the subject of Agricultural Schools and report to the next Legislature. The Rev. Edward Hitchcock, President of Amherst College, was one of this commission, and being then in Europe, Mr. Wilder guaranteed his expenses in investigating the schools abroad, which were finally paid by the State. Pres. Hitchcock furnished materials for a Report to the next Legislature, with the statistics of 352 schools in Europe. This report and these efforts were the first seeds of the Agricultural College, which is now located at Amherst, and of which Mr. W. is the first named trustee.

Having been appointed by Gov. Briggs a Commissioner at the Exhibition of all Nations in the Crystal Palace at New York, he attended on that occasion. A similar compliment was paid him in 1850, when he was appointed as Chairman of the Commission in behalf of Massachusetts for the World's Fair in London, but his engagements were such that he could not leave home.

In 1852, he prepared a circular, under the auspices of the Massachusetts Board of Agriculture, of which he was President, for a National Convention of Agriculturists. It was signed by himself

and ten other Presidents of different State Societies ; and a meeting
was called at Washington, June 24, 1852. One hundred and fifty
delegates representing twenty-three States responded in person to the
call. They met in the rooms of the Smithsonian Institution, and the
United States Agricultural Society having been organized, Col. Wilder
was chosen President. Among other matters in his Address on that
occasion, he said :

" Gentlemen, we are here to advance an art coeval with the existence of the human
race—an art which employs eighteen millions of our population, and four-fifths of all the
capital in our fair land—an art which lies at the very foundation of national and individual
prosperity and wealth, the basis of commerce, of manufactures and of industrial pursuits.
We are an agricultural people ; our habits, our dispositions are rural. I rejoice that it is
so, and I pray that it may ever continue to be so. Our country embraces every variety of
soil, and is capable of producing most of the products of the torrid and the temperate
zones ; and with a suitable application of science to this art, there is no reason why American agriculture may not sustain competition with that of any nation on the civilized globe."

On the conclusion of business, a large number of the delegates in
procession called on President Fillmore, and on Mr. Webster, received
their congratulations, and invited their influence and co-operation.

The next annual meeting of the United States Agricultural Society
was at Washington, Feb. 21, 1853. They met in sorrow. The illustrious friend of Agriculture was no more, and in his Address at that
meeting, President Wilder paid a noble tribute to the memory of his
departed friend :

" 'The Marshfield Farmer' is also numbered with the mighty dead. He was a farmer,
the son of a farmer, and the noblest production of American soil ! His majestic form, his
mountain brow, and expressive countenance, his deep, yet melodious voice, his whole
person eloquent in every step and act, are bright visions on which we delight to dwell.

" We fondly cherish the remembrance of him as he appeared in this assembly at the
organization of our Society, and in the cordial manner in which he saluted the worthy
representative of the immortal Washington, the 'Farmer of Arlington.' We love to think
of his subsequent reception of us at his hospitable mansion in the city, and of the close
of his eloquent address, and especially of his friendly benediction—' Brother farmers, I
shall remember you, and the occasion which has called us together. I invoke for you a
safe return to your homes. I invoke for you an abundant harvest ; and if we meet not
again in time, I trust that hereafter we shall meet in a more genial clime, and under a
kindlier sun.'

" Yes, sainted patriot, *there* in those celestial fields, where the sickle of the great Reaper
shall no more cut down the wise and the good, we hope at last to meet thee—*there*, where
thy brilliant star shall shine with purer effulgence, and where the high and glorious aspi-
rations of thy soul shall be forever realized ! "

The First Exhibition under the superintendence of this Society was
a National Horse Show at Springfield, Mass., Oct. 19—21, 1853. Great
preparations were made by the liberal citizens of that place who had
solicited its co-operation. The meeting was on grounds of twenty

acres ; a track for the course, and a gallery for spectators with rising tiers of seats, were provided. A large crowd of spectators assembled. Five hundred fine horses advanced into the arena, some richly caparisoned, and the procession of gallant steeds and riders passed like a pageant before the eyes of the multitude. Several thousands of dollars were distributed in premiums. Speeches were made at the banquet by Abbot Lawrence, our late minister to the Court of St. James, Gov. Seymour of New York, Gov. Colby of New Hampshire, John Minor Botts of Virginia, Rev. F. D. Huntington of Boston, and others. Nor was the equestrian exhibition without an Address from the President. Mr. Lawrence, in speaking of the exceeding value of the horse, made this remark :

"We talk in these modern times of the steam engine and the telegraph as the great civilizers of man. But the horse has been a greater civilizer than either the steam engine or the electric telegraph."

The Society held a National Cattle Show at Springfield, Ohio, Oct. 25—27, 1854. It was remarkable for the superiority of the cattle.

A premium of $500 having been offered for the best herd consisting of a bull and five cows, the excellence of the herds on the list was so great that the judges, after some days deliberation, were unable to come to a decision and withheld it. An offer was made to divide equally between the proprietors of the two best herds, but one of them (Brutus J. Clay) declined, saying emphatically, "I came here for the honor, and not for money."

At the banquet, which was honored by the presence of ladies, there were among the guests, Gov. Wright of Indiana, now minister to Prussia, Cassius M. Clay, now minister to Russia, and his brother Brutus J. Clay ; Col. L. F. Allen, of New York ; Hon. Chauncey Holcomb, of Delaware ; Colonels Saunders and Williams, of Kentucky, and other gentlemen of rank, with delegates from many States and from Canada ; and by the side of the President sat the venerable Madam Warder, of Springfield, Ohio—a noble lady of the Old School.

This exhibition is described in the President's Address :

"This is the first National Exhibition of Cattle ever held in America, and I do but express the common sentiment of the assemblage, when I say that it has more than realized the anticipations of all concerned. It has been eminently successful, and alike honorable to the citizens of Springfield, to the State of Ohio, and to the great Republic. There have been 200 entries at this exhibition ; and it has seldom or never been the happiness of man to behold such samples in one show, and larger premiums have been offered for the encouragement 'of this department of American husbandry, than ever before excited competition."

Gov. Wright, after speaking with admiration of the Cattle Show, concluded by offering this sentiment :

"*The First United States Agricultural Banquet.* A Union this day of the citizens of Eighteen States. May these associations continue to increase and multiply, until we shall meet at these annual festivals the citizens of each State, District and Territory of this Republic, and greet each other not as members of different sections of the country, but as citizens, known and recognized by the prouder and higher name of an AMERICAN CITIZEN."

The Third Exhibition of the United States Agricultural Society was held in Boston, Oct. 23—27, 1855. Mr. Wilder, being desirous to have one exhibition near his home, had been seeking for suitable grounds, but could find none until the middle of August, when he called on the Mayor and offered to select Boston for this purpose, if the city would level and seed down the land just made, easterly of Harrison avenue, where the new City Hospital has since been erected. They agreed to get it ready, and expended in the preparation $15,000. A square of thirty acres or more was enclosed by a high, strong fence, and with imposing and handsome entrances. It was furnished with seats rising one above another like a gallery on the western side, where 10,000 spectators could be accommodated. Pens and stalls were arranged on the other sides, and capacious tents were located in the middle of the grounds. Gentlemen in Boston pledged $20,000 to defray the expenses, and the old " Massachusetts Society for the Promotion of Agriculture " generously contributed $1000 towards the same. The President in his Address thus describes the place :

" One of the most interesting incidents of this exhibition relates to the spot on which it is held. This whole territory is land redeemed from Neptune's dominion. Here modern enterprise has literally fulfilled the words of Scripture, and has said to the surrounding hills, ' Be ye plucked up and cast into the sea ; ' and they have moved in obedience to its command. Here, where but yesterday rolled the ocean's wave ; here, in the middle of the nineteenth century, and in the midst of this populous and flourishing city, the National Agricultural Society has come up with its flocks and herds, pitched its tents, and invited you to unite in celebrating the triumphs of art over nature, and to witness the achievements of science in a most important department of husbandry."

The show of animals was uncommonly good. This display of the wealth of the country lasted five days, during which, under the vigilance and energy of Gen. John S. Tyler, Chief Marshal, perfect order and good feeling prevailed, as the vast multitude swayed from place to place, not an accident having occurred to mar the pleasures of the occasion. Over the pavilion waved the flags of England, France and other powers, while the stars and stripes hung among them in all their glory.

It was truly a sublime spectacle—so many fair ladies and men of rank and talent from different States, had assembled to do honor to the honest yeomanry of the land, who there saw the labor of the hand respected, and the cultivation of the soil encouraged. Twenty States and many State Agricultural Societies were represented by delegates. From sixty to seventy thousand visitors passed the gates one day, when the receipts were $13,000. Ten thousand dollars were assigned for premiums. A corps of reporters from the leading newspapers in the country attended this exhibition, and an elegant engraving of it and of the Prize animals may be found in the Journal of the United States Agricultural Society for 1855. The total receipts were nearly $40,000.

Among the men of note at the banquet, at which there were 2000 persons, were Gov. Henry J. Gardner, Mayor J. V. C. Smith of Massachusetts; Gov. Hoppin of Rhode Island, Hon. Morton McMichael of Philadelphia, Edward Everett, Robert C. Winthrop, John C. Gray, Boston, Ex-Governor King of New York, B. B. French, Washington, Col. Thompson, President of the Board of Agriculture of Canada, and others. Rev. Dr. S. K. Lothrop asked the blessing.

After dinner, the President delivered an Address; and when he concluded, the whole assembly rose and gave him three cordial cheers. He then gave a sentiment, to which Gov. Gardner responded in a brief and appropriate speech, wherein he remarked:

"It is true, as you say in the toast you have just uttered, that our fathers were farmers, and in connection, sir, it is also true that liberty is the tree which they planted, and which has flourished to the present day. Go where you will, all history teaches that in agricultural communities you will find the deepest devotion to the spirit of liberty." [Cheers.]

The speeches on this occasion from Mr. McMichael, Edward Everett, and some others, were remarkable. A few extracts are given.

Mr. McMichael:

"Mr. President: As I looked yesterday, on the gratifying exhibition made among the triple hills of your beautiful Boston, like his Excellency, the Governor, I too was reminded of those ancient days, when, from all the isles of Greece, the people gathered to a periodical festival, foremost among whose attractions were the achievements of the race-course and the ring. . . . . . . Mr. President, the Greek, with all his elegance and refinement; with all his philosophy and learning; with all his exquisite appreciation of poetry, and music, and painting, and sculpture, and statuary, had no adequate conception of the true value and just position of woman, and admitted her to no participation, unless in exceptional cases, in his higher pursuits and graver occupations. . . . . You, sir, have been guided by a wiser and better influence, and recognizing that social equality of the sexes, which reason and revelation alike teach us, you have thrown your gates wide open to the maids and the matrons of the community, you have given them due precedence as well in the spectacles as at the banquet, and in the bright, the thoughtful, the eloquent faces, which at this moment turn towards me, I perceive the visible tokens of the illimitable advance which our Christian has made over heathen civilization."

Mr. Everett, comparing our Indian corn to California gold :

" Far different the case with our Atlantic gold; it does not perish when consumed, but, by a nobler alchemy than that of Paracelsus, is transmuted in consumption to a higher life. 'Perish in consumption,' did the old miser say ? 'Thou fool, that which thou sowest is not quickened except it die.' The burning pen of inspiration, ranging heaven and earth for a similitude, to convey to our poor minds some not inadequate idea of the mighty doctrine of the resurrection, can find no symbol so expressive ' as bare grain it may chance of wheat or some other grain.' To-day a senseless plant, to-morrow it is human bone and muscle, vein and artery, sinew and nerve ; beating pulse, heaving lungs, toiling, ah, sometimes, overtoiling brain. Last June, it sucked from the cold breast of the earth the watery nourishment of its distending sap-vessels ; and now it clothes the manly form with warm, cordial flesh ; quivers and thrills with the five-fold of sense ; purveys and ministers to the higher mystery of thought. Heaped up in your granaries this week, the next it will strike in the stalwart arm, and glow in the blushing cheek, and flash in the beaming eye ;—till we learn at last to realize that the slender stalk, which we have seen shaken by the summer breeze, bending in the cornfield under the yellow burden of harvest, is indeed the ' staff of life,' which, since the world began, has supported the toiling and struggling myriads of humanity on the mighty pilgrimage of being." . . . .

And with regard to this Exhibition, he observes :

" But when I look around upon your exhibition—the straining course—the crowded, bustling ring—the motion, the life, the fire—the immense crowds of ardent youth and emulous manhood, assembled from almost every part of the country, actors or spectators of the scene—I feel that it is hardly the place for quiet, old-fashioned folks, accustomed to quiet, old-fashioned ways. I feel somewhat like the Doge of Genoa, whom the imperious mandate of Louis XIV. had compelled to come to Versailles, and who, after surveying and admiring its marvels, exclaimed, that he wondered at every thing he saw, and most of all at finding himself there."

Mr. Winthrop related an important fact in our agricultural history :

" The Philadelphia Record of Dec. 5, 1785, sets forth, that a letter was received ' from the Hon. William Drayton, Esq., Chairman of the Committee of the *South Carolina Society of Agriculture*, inclosing a few copies of their address and rules, and soliciting a correspondence with this Society.' This letter was dated Nov. 2, 1785, and leaves no doubt, therefore, that South Carolina had established a State Agricultural Society at least seven years before Massachusetts. It is certainly a striking circumstance, that the year of its establishment was the very year in which the first five bales of cotton ever exported from America, were entered at Liverpool, and were actually seized at the Custom House, on the ground that no such thing as cotton had ever been grown, or could ever be grown in

America! Indigo was then a staple export of Carolina, of which hardly a plant is now found upon her soil, and of which not a pound is exported. Truly, Sir, there have been revolutions in the vegetable kingdom, within a century past, hardly less wonderful than those of the civil and political world."

Ex-Governor John A. King, of New York, in the course of his remarks paid this compliment to the President:

" I have also the honor to belong to the same Society to which our distinguished President belongs—the United States Agricultural Society. I have served with him also in that capacity; and I am here to say in your presence, and to his honor, that I know no fitter, no abler, more efficient officer for that distinguished post. At home and abroad, the same man, the same power, the same vigor, and the same intellect, are all brought to bear on the great cause which we are here assembled to celebrate.

" I came to assist in this great celebration; and well have I been repaid for it. I have witnessed a scene upon this made land, such as no man in this country has ever before witnessed. I have seen, not only the most beautiful specimens of animals of all characters, but I have seen the noblest assemblage of the noblest animal—man. I have seen one hundred thousand persons, well dressed, intelligent, and capable of every thing that man can be called upon to do—here assembled to witness that which the Society, under his administration, has been able to produce before you; orderly, quiet, and requiring no police, no bayonets, but showing the influence and power of education, here, in its greatest stronghold, New England." . . . . .

The Fourth Annual Exhibition was held at Philadelphia, Oct. 7—11, 1856. The grounds were on the banks of the Schuylkill—an area of forty acres—with twenty entrances, at each of which the daily visitors were recorded by a register. There were 750 stalls for cattle, 300 for horses, and 150 for swine and sheep. A track for horses half a mile long and forty feet wide, was laid at the expense of $1200; besides a carriage road a mile in circumference. There were ornamental gateways at each end of the enclosure, and architectural structures flanked with towers; and at the north a bridge sixty feet long and twenty-five broad spanned a deep ravine. Inside on the green sward stood an immense marquee, numerous tents and structures. Fronting the whole, was a balcony with rising tiers of seats a thousand feet in length, sufficient for six thousand ladies and gentlemen; while in the centre of the area on a tall flag-staff waved a banner, with the inscription, UNITED STATES AGRICULTURAL SOCIETY. Westward of this, an elegant iron fountain refreshed the air with its lofty snow-white showers; and to add one more charm to the romantic scene, the grand iron track, which unites Philadelphia to the far West, lay in the back ground of the picture, winding its way through the woods, while ever and anon the locomotive seemed to respond to the occasion.

C

The Municipal Authorities, Board of Trade, and Society of Philadelphia for Promoting Agriculture, did themselves honor in these magnificent arrangements. Such was the concourse of visitors that $38,000 were received for entrances, and $14,000 distributed in premiums.

The banquet was graced with the beauty and fashion of Philadelphia and the country. There were twenty-eight tables, at which were seated more than two thousand ladies and gentlemen. Bishop Potter, of Pennsylvania, invoked a blessing, and Bishop McCrosky, of Illinois, returned thanks. Then the President addressed the assembly. The following extract will illustrate the occasion :

" The lively interest manifested in this exhibition, and the great concourse of persons attending it, afford ample evidence of the high esteem in which agriculture and rural arts are held. It will have been witnessed, should the pleasant weather continue, by more than two hundred thousand people, and it has been pronounced, by competent judges, the most interesting ever held on this side the Atlantic. The number of entries has been very large. In stock, it has embraced some of the finest specimens of the different breeds, which this or any other country can afford. The latter, with the display of implements and productions of the soil and the arts, reflects great honor upon the contributors, the Society and the country."

Among the guests were Mayor Vaux of Philadelphia, Gov. Pollock of Pennsylvania, the Clergy of the Diocese then in session in the city, Gov. Price of New Jersey, George Washington P. Custis, "the Farmer of Arlington," the Hon. Josiah Quincy, Jr. of Massachusetts, Hon. A. B. Conger of New York, Judge Robeson of New Jersey, Hon. William Meredith of Philadelphia, with numerous delegates from the State Societies. The first speaker was Gov. Pollock. A few extracts only will be given, as the Journal of the United States Agricultural Society, Vol. 3, 1856–7, contains a full history of these celebrations.

Gov. Pollock made remarks worthy of being preserved in letters of gold :

" The farmer is, in and of himself, independent. He is God's nobleman. Labor! let it be dignified! let it be honored! Labor is honest in all its associations. Labor is honorable—dignified. Fear not to touch its hard hand or its brawny arm. [Applause.] I would, if I had time, direct your attention more particularly to this fact. We must educate labor. We must educate our sons to make mechanics; we must convert our colleges into the workshops—into the harvest fields. We must make them understand that they are men. Professions are crowded—pressed to the earth. We want a race of God's noblemen. Educate labor! Educate, honor, dignify it, and in its turn it will educate and dignify the men who employ it."

He was followed by Hon. A. B. Conger, Ex-President of the New York Agricultural Society, who speaking of the occasion says—

" I cannot withhold the expression of wonder which I have experienced in witnessing this exhibition. I doubt whether there are many Americans at heart, who could withhold an expression of honest pride, as in surveying the countless productions gathered together in this immense arena, they have witnessed the trophies of American skill applied to American Agriculture. Go with me, and your pulse will be quickened as you cast your eye upon that machine, which a few years ago startled the old world and made them acknowledge that American ingenuity had produced the most successful reaper known."

Extract from Mr. Custis's speech :

" And now let me say a single word before I conclude. In all my public addresses, amid all varieties of those to whom I have spoken publicly for two generations, I have always called up the story of those revolutionary times. The sun shines sweetly on you now, my countrymen, but remember that there was a bitter storm in Valley Forge. You glory in your liberties; you run riot in prosperity—remember the days of '76. Bear in mind the services and sufferings of those who made you what you are; drop a tear to their memory and transmit their fame to the remotest generation. And you Pennsylvania—you who have the temple of Independence here in your bosom on the one side, and Valley Forge on the other—Go to those decayed and memorable instances which are left of that ancient encampment—go and mark there *pretium libertatis* —the price of liberty. See what it cost, and remember with undying gratitude the names of those who won for you so much honor in those trying times. I must now bid you a kind adieu, and when I say farewell, it is a valedictory : I shall see you no more."

A letter, dated Oct. 6, 1856, to the President from Hon. Robert C. Winthrop, was read, in which he regretted that he could not be present, and observes :

" In addition to the lively interest which I should have taken in the occasion personally, I had relied on fulfilling the trust imposed upon me by my colleagues, of representing the old ' Massachusetts Society for the Promotion of Agriculture,' and of offering in their behalf, to the United States Society, a renewed assurance of co-operation and sympathy in the great objects for which both are associated."

The following toast, enclosed in his letter, was then read :

" *The Farmers of Pennsylvania and of the United States.* May they adopt and steadily pursue such a policy in regard both to Agriculture and every other American interest, as will prevent our beloved country from ever being clothed in *weeds.*"

The President then announced a representative of an illustrious ancestor of New England, Hon. Josiah Quincy, Jr., and who the past season had witnessed the great exhibition at Paris. Mr. Quincy thus spoke :

" Fellow citizens : Perhaps there never was a more unjust accusation made against a man, than was made by the gentleman who preceded me, who declared that in Boston, after dinner, we always have a specimen of Ciceronian eloquence. I assure you, gentlemen, that if Mr. Winthrop, who signed the letter, which has been read by the President, had had the honor of addressing you, you might have had a specimen of that eloquence.

" But really, Mr. President, I wish, in rising to address this assembly, to say that I possess the great advantage that one of my ancestors had, who, a hundred and one years ago, came from Boston to Philadelphia for the purpose of making a speech. . . . . . My ancestor came here and had occasion to address the legislature of Pennsylvania, but being like his successor a very modest man, he called upon a member to assist him, and that member happened to be no less than a runaway apprentice from Boston, Benjamin Franklin. (Great applause.) What was the worst of it all, this Benjamin Franklin tells us in his autobiography that being consulted by Mr. Quincy upon that subject, he [Franklin] dictated his speech for him, and not only dictated his speech for him, but he put it down in his autobiography, so that all mankind might forever know that he did not make the speech that he addressed to the Pennsylvanians one hundred years ago."

A National Trial of Reapers and Mowers was held by the United States Agricultural Society, at Syracuse, N. Y., July, 1857, and continued for eight days. The Board of Judges consisted of one from each of twenty-four States. Forty-two machines were entered for competition. The interest was intense. The reports of the judges, the award of premiums, and the illustration of machines, may be found in the Transactions of the Society for that year. This Exhibition was witnessed by the Governors of New York and Kentucky, the New York State Agricultural Society in a body, and numerous State representatives. The trial of labor-saving implements, and the elaborate report of the judges, constitute one of the most important and useful acts in the history of the Society, as will appear by the remarks of the President, Mr. Wilder, in his Address on the occasion :

" The commendatory announcement by the press of this exhibition throughout the land, and the gathering of this concourse of our intelligent yeomanry, together with inventors and manufacturers from this and other countries, the lightning and the press ready to convey the report of the progress and result of this experiment to millions of readers anxiously in waiting for it, bear concurrent testimony to the universal interest, general utility and paramount importance of this trial.

" When we consider the great extent of our fields of grass and grain, the vast agricultural resources of our rapidly increasing national farm, the labor, capital and intelligence requisite for the development of these, the diversion of human energy to other departments of industry, the question comes home with augmented force, how are our bountiful harvests to be gathered, with a suitable regard to the economy of labor, and to the preservation of the crops? There is but one satisfactory reply—*by the improved implements of husbandry—by a substitution of the labor of domestic animals for that of mankind, and ere long by the application of ' steam wrought and steam impelled machinery.' "

The Fifth Annual Exhibition of the United States Agricultural Society was held at Louisville, Kentucky, and commencing Aug. 31, 1857, it lasted five days. Thirty thousand dollars were guaranteed by public-spirited citizens to defray the expenses, twelve thousand dollars offered as premiums, and an area of fifty acres three miles out of the city tendered by the Western Agricultural and Mechanical Association for the occasion. Spacious buildings, saloons, and a large marquee, halls, tents and stalls, had been erected ; a course for the horses laid out, of half a mile in length ; and an immense amphitheatre 210 feet in diameter, with rising tiers of seats for spectators, modelled after the ancient Coliseum of Rome, roofed and ornamented with fluted columns, evinced the warm and patriotic spirit which that festival awakened. Twenty-seven States appeared by representatives, and forty-eight Agricultural and Horticultural Societies sent their delegates ; and reporters of forty-two newspapers were courteously cared for by Maj. Ben Perley Poore, the efficient Secretary of the Society. Such were the preparations in Louisville for this magnificent celebration. The heavens too were propitious—a succession of autumnal days when the sky appears in her deepest blue and the earth in her loveliest colors.

But we can only take a bird's-eye view, and see a vast concourse of spectators, some in groups gazing on every variety of cattle and domestic animals—others admiring horses of high pedigree, and especially three full-blood Arabians—here a crowd pressing into a machine-shop to observe some labor-saving invention—and there the lovers of fruit and flowers eyeing one rare collection after another—and then behold a magnificent display of the Durham, Devon and fat cattle, in the arena of the amphitheatre, and then a grand cavalcade of splendid horses, passing by those rising tiers crowned with the beauty and fashion of the West. But the reader must be referred to the Journal of the United States Agricultural Society, Vol. iii.

Of the many guests only a few names can be given : Mayor Pitcher of Louisville, Gov. Morehead of Kentucky, Ex-Governors Wickliffe, Powell and Helm ; John C. Breckinridge, Vice President of the United States ; James Guthrie, Secretary of the United States Treasury; Gen. Tilghman of Maryland ; Judge Huntington of the Supreme Court, Indiana ; Gen. Wilson, Iowa ; Col. Barrett, Missouri ; C. L. Flint, Secretary of the Massachusetts Agricultural Board ; Frederic Smyth, since Gov. of New Hampshire ; Colonels Mallory and Buchanan. Speeches were made by many gentlemen.

Mr. Wilder :

"One of the most hopeful and delightful features of these national jubilees relates to the genial influences which they exert on all classes of society, associating them together with friendly greetings, and making them one in interest and one in affection. . . . . .

"My heart is no stranger to that interest which has brought this immense concourse together—to the inspiration of that sentiment which I trust will ever animate the hearts of the American people—to those patriotic emotions which merge all sectional jealousies and party distinctions in a general desire for the public weal.

"We come from different and distant portions of our country. I am from the home of the Puritans, but I am most happy to meet you here in this land of cavaliers and chivalry—and here upon the broad platform of good citizenship, to unite my influence with yours in furtherance of our common cause, and in cementing the bonds of union—to join hands with you, Sir, the Governor of the Commonwealth of Kentucky, and through you with this assembly, in exemplification of the glorious inscription on the seal of your State: UNITED WE STAND, DIVIDED WE FALL."

To which Gov. Morehead replied :

"You have spoken, Mr. President, of the motto engraved on our coat of arms, 'United we stand, divided we fall.' Let me tell you, sir, that it is still more indelibly engraved on the heart of every Kentuckian. We do not allow ourselves to argue upon the subject. We never yet realized the possibility of dividing. Devotion to the Union is not the result of reason alone, but with us it is a holy sentiment of the heart. I have an abiding conviction that God will preserve us for a nobler end than this. But if he should punish us by the infliction of such a calamity, the work should be done in a paroxysm of frenzy when reason was dethroned and madness ruled the hour. May God avert from us the desolation and ruin which such an event would scatter over a smiling land. May the time never arrive when the motto—'United we stand, divided we fall,' shall grow dim in our hearts."

"The Grand closing Cavalcade. The bell was sounded for the last time—the band struck up the National Anthem—the gates were thrown open—and the cavalcade of premium horses entered the arena, decked with their ribbons of victory. Matched horses in harness, rockaway and buggy horses, stallions, mares and geldings, fillies, ponies, trotters, pacers, followed in regular succession, passing around and around the arena to the inspiring notes of the band, cheered by the waving of ladies' handkerchiefs, and by the continued shouts of the gentlemen. There were seventy-eight magnificent premium animals together, moving around like the ever-varying hues of the kaleidoscope, and forming a fitting *finale* to the displays in the amphitheatre. The great heart of the assembled multitude beat with pride and satisfaction, and all seemed to go from the amphitheatre at last with reluctance, as if unwilling to quit the scene of so much unalloyed satisfaction."

The Sixth Annual Meeting of the United States Agricultural Society was held at Washington, Feb. 13, 1858. Pres. Wilder spoke with much feeling and respect of the death of Mr. Custis.

"The venerable Mr. Custis was well known to us as the 'Farmer of Arlington,' an honorable title conferred upon him on this platform by Daniel Webster, at the organization of this Society, and one by which his name will descend to posterity. He was present at each of its annual meetings, occupying a seat on the right of the chair; and at the close of each, pronouncing, by my request, a farewell address and benediction. By his death the last representative member of the immortal Washington has passed away. The following were his touching and prophetic words at the close of our last meeting:

" 'The time has come for me to say *Farewell*—and when a man on whose head rests the snows of seventy-six winters, bids you farewell, the probabilities are that it will be a long farewell. You will now return to your homes with hearts cheered and hands strengthened by this mutual communion, and this brotherhood of farmers from all parts of our great country. And you will come up to our National Capital another year, each one with fresh cause of encouragement for the rest, each one with more information and labors, which he will interchange with his fellows, and thus scatter broadcast over the land. And as you come up from all portions of the country—from the classic grounds where our fathers died—let your hands labor for the prosperity of the country they bought with their blood.

" 'And now, Gentlemen of the United States Agricultural Society—Farewell! Go back to your homes, and tell your friends what has been done at this meeting for the cause of Agriculture, and encourage them as you have been encouraged. Continue your devotion to this bulwark of our country, continue inviolate our great Constitution, obey our self-imposed laws, preserve our blessed Union, and our Republic will be immortal!' "

In conclusion he declined a re-election, and remarked :

" Among the considerations which have prevailed with me was a desire to reciprocate your kindness, and to conform my action to your judgment—that my official service was important to the establishment and success of our Society. These objects have now been accomplished. The United States Agricultural Society is a recognized national institution. Wherever its exhibitions are held we are sure to meet, not only gentlemen of all professions, but thousands of our intelligent yeomanry. The Society has now attained a standing that will ensure its perpetuity and usefulness, and a name that will descend to future generations. My resignation, therefore, which I now for the third time tender you, cannot be prejudicial to its interests."

Gen. Tench Tilghman, of Maryland, was chosen in his place, and the following Resolutions were then passed :

" *Whereas*, the Hon. Marshall P. Wilder, of Massachusetts, who has for years so eminently distinguished himself by his exertions in promoting the cause of terraculture, has declined a further re-election to the office of President of this Society, which he has filled since its creation, with ability, industry and outlay of his private means :

" Therefore, *Resolved*, That his name be placed on the roll of honorary members of the United States Agricultural Society ; and that the Executive Committee are instructed to present him a suitable testimonial as a mark of the approbation of this Society, for the energy, time and money which he has expended in advancing its interests, and raising it to the position which it now occupies."

Mr. Wilder replied—

" Long may it live and be a blessing to our country, and may its last days be its best days. For six successive terms you have honored me with your confidence as President of this Association—an office which I esteem as one of the highest and most honorable that could be conferred on me. For each of the last two years I have tendered you my resignation, but have yielded to your urgent solicitation, and have discharged the duties of the position at great personal sacrifice and to the best of my ability."

A vote was passed, appropriating $250 as a testimonial, with which an elegant Tea Service was obtained.

In his Valedictory he remarks :

" Endowed from my youth with a love for rural life and rural taste, I have but obeyed the instincts of my nature in devoting such time, ability and means as I could command to the cultivation of the earth. In the incipient measures towards the formation of this Society, in all efforts for its encouragement, and in whatever I have been able to do for the promotion of the general cause, I have only been following the leadings of Providence and the promptings of my own conscience."

At the next Annual Meeting, the "*Large Gold Medal of Honor*," valued at $150, was awarded, with this inscription : "Awarded to Hon. Marshall P. Wilder, FOUNDER, FIRST PRESIDENT AND CONSTANT PATRON."

Thus closed Mr. Wilder's administration, wherein he had presided and delivered addresses at all of the annual meetings in Washington, and exhibitions in the various States.

A Festival of the Sons of New Hampshire resident in Boston, was held on the 7th of November, 1849. It was an imposing spectacle, and deserves a description far beyond these limits. They met at the State House. A large procession was formed, and moved through several streets, each county with its banner. Nearly fifteen hundred persons sat down at thirty tables in the spacious Railroad Hall over the Fitchburg Depot, which was adorned with pictures, sketches and emblematic mottoes. It was an occasion calculated to call up sweet memories of the past, and fill the mind with pictures of lakes and mountains, highlands and valleys, where the fresh and joyous days of boyhood were pased ; and perhaps, there was not one whose soul did not thrill at the thought of "the school-house—the school-house everywhere in New Hampshire," which Mr. Webster so beautifully described. Here he sat as President, with the Vice Presidents, of whom Mr. Wilder was first. On his right and left were statesmen, clergymen, and men of high rank. And it was here that Mr. Webster made one of his brilliant speeches, touching the historic character of New Hampshire in the Indian wars and in the Revolution, and where the great men of the Granite State stood out in bold relief as the patriots of other days. He was followed by Judge Woodbury, then of the Supreme Court of the United States, Mr. Wilder, Mayor Bigelow, Judge Joel Parker, Gen. H. A. S. Dearborn, Ex-Governor Henry Hubbard, John P. Hale, Charles B. Goodrich, William Plummer, James Wilson, Levi Chamberlain and others. Poems by George Kent, Esq., and Mrs. Sarah J. Hale, with other poetic effusions, enlivened the entertainment.

A full account of the Festival was published in 1850, ornamented with portraits of Webster, Woodbury and Wilder ; the last of whom, speaking of New Hampshire, observed :

"She has raised men, *great men*, and had she performed no other service, this alone were sufficient to associate her name with Sparta and Athens, in the history of mankind. Her Stark, to whom you have so happily alluded, Mr. President, was a modern Leonidas, and among her orators, no one could hesitate to point out a Demosthenes!"

The Sons of New Hampshire were again called together on the 29th of October, 1852. The nation was in mourning—the Festival ordered for Nov. 18th, was postponed. Daniel Webster, their President, was no more! He died at Marshfield, Oct. 24, 1852; and a delegation of this association attended his funeral. But a more public and general expression of their sorrow was manifested on the 30th day of November—a day set apart in Boston for his obsequies.

On the morning of that day, a Select Committee, with the Hon. John S. Wells, President of the Senate, at their head, having been appointed by the Legislature of New Hampshire, arrived at the Lowell Depot, and were received by the Sons of New Hampshire, and addressed by Mr. W., President on the occasion, who observed:

"A mighty one has fallen! Our elder brother, New Hampshire's favorite son, is no more. All that was mortal of Daniel Webster, the great expounder of constitutional authority and national rights, has been consigned to the bosom of his mother earth.

"The loss to us, to the country and to the world, is irreparable. The whole nation mourns; our city is hung in the drapery of woe, and 'the mourners go about the streets.'

"But in this hour of trial and sorrow, let us not forget that our loss is his unspeakable gain. While we mourn, let us thank God that he was spared to us so long—that he was enabled to do so much for us, and for the cause of universal freedom and humanity, and that his sun was permitted to go down unclouded, and shining in the greatness of its strength.

"Gentlemen, it is not my province to pronounce his eulogy; that duty will be performed by abler men and more gifted lips. Daniel Webster is dead! We shall see that majestic form no more! But his fame is immortal. It is registered on the hearts of his grateful countrymen. Yes, and it shall be transmitted unsullied and untarnished through all coming ages; and when the monumental marble shall have crumbled into dust, it shall '*still live!*' It shall live forever."

They proceeded then to the State House, and in the Representatives' Hall the Select Committee were introduced by Mr. Wilder to Gov. Boutwell, where speeches of condolence were exchanged. They then joined the great procession under a military escort to Faneuil Hall, which was draped in the emblems of sorrow. There an eloquent and heart-stirring Eulogy was delivered by the Hon. George S. Hillard. Boston, since she has been a city, never saw a more solemn day—stores closed—numerous public and private residences festooned in black—flags at half-mast—muffled drums—the long procession—the noiseless, respectful mass of people, who lined the streets—all

7

seemed to speak a deep feeling of sorrow at the obsequies of a great man.

The Second Festival of the Sons of New Hampshire was held at the Railroad Hall of the Fitchburg Depot, Nov. 2, 1853. The preparations were similar to the first. Thirteen hundred partook of the banquet, and Mr. Wilder presided. In his address he reminded the assembly that Samuel Appleton, Joseph Bell, Henry A. S. Dearborn, John McNiel and John C. Merrill, names on the roll of the Vice Presidents, were gone. He then touches the deepest cords of sorrow in remembrance of the First Festival.

"We have to mourn the loss of two distinguished sons then present, who will never be forgotten: LEVI WOODBURY, who entered early into public life, and whose eminent services both in New Hampshire and Massachusetts, and in the counsels and judiciary of the nation, have won for him imperishable fame; and last, not least, DANIEL WEBSTER, whose official relation to this body demands a grateful tribute to his memory. His surpassing eloquence on that memorable night will ever remain among the choicest treasures of our memories. Who of us can ever forget the manner in which he stood up on this spot, the great champion of universal freedom and national rights, and before the civilized world, exhorted the Russian Autocrat to respect the law of nations; and warning him, if he did not, in the following emphatic and terrible language:—'There is something on earth greater than arbitrary or despotic power. The lightning has its power, and the whirlwind has its power, and the earthquake has its power; but there is something among men more capable of shaking despotic thrones than lightning, whirlwind or earthquake—that is the excited and aroused indignation of the whole civilized world.'

"The voice that pronounced this anathema is silent; but the sentiments which it then uttered are now shaking to their very foundations the thrones of Europe. Who of us can forget his majestic form and mountain brow, as he then stood before us the very impersonation of greatness and power—

'Like some tall cliff that lifts its awful form,
Swells from the vale and midway leaves the storm.'

And in view of the closing hour of his life, fringed with the rosy tints of a fairer to-morrow; in view of his serenity of mind, his Christian resignation, and his hope of a glorious immortality, may we not, with little modification, add the other lines of this beautiful stanza—

'Though round his breast the rolling clouds were spread,
Eternal sunshine settles on his head.'

"Aye, brothers, in that serene upper sky, to which we trust they have ascended, where we hope to meet them at last, and beneath the rainbow about the throne, to celebrate a more enduring and glorious festival."

"What a tide of hallowed associations cluster around the homes of our childhood—the hand which rocked our cradle—the parents who nurtured us—the rocks and hills—the brooks and vales—the district school-house—the village church—the family mansion, and—

'The old elm, that hath been our joy
From the very childhood up.'

"The emotions which these remembrances awaken, flow from the purest fountains of the soul. Cease to remember the land of our birth! Not while the granite of the heaven-piercing hills shall endure—not while gratitude shall be the grateful language of the heart.

'Land of our fathers, whereso'er we roam,
Land of our birth, to us thou still art home.'"

The next meeting of the Sons of New Hampshire was called to receive the Second Regiment of New Hampshire Volunteers, who arrived June 20, 1861, on their route to the army. They were 1200 strong, commanded by Col. Gilbert Marston. The Boston Cadets escorted them in their march through several streets to Music Hall, where sixteen hundred persons partook of a handsome collation. Mr. W., who presided, in conclusion remarked :

"Mr. Commander and Fellow Soldiers : You go forth to support the Constitution which our immortal Webster labored so zealously to defend. [Cheers.] To preserve that Union which he declared should be perpetual; and here, uniting our voices with yours, we solemnly declare that, sink or swim, live or die, this glorious Union, purchased by the blood of our fathers, shall not be divided. That in the future as in the past, we will have but one country, one government, one destiny ; and here, too, on the altar of our common country, God helping us, we most reverently swear, in the language of our sainted brother, that this Union shall be *one and inseparable,* now and forever !"

"May the God of battles speed, prosper and protect you on your way ; and whether you are permitted to return to your happy homes again, or whether you fall in defence of that flag, encrimsoned in the blood of patriots and martyrs, your names shall be enshrined in our hearts with grateful remembrance, more precious than king or potentate can boast, more durable than sculptured marble or monumental stone."

The 4th of July, 1855, and the 225th Anniversary of the settlement of Dorchester, were celebrated in that town by a union of parties. It was a day to be long remembered. The cloudless sky—the grand Pavilion on Webster Hill—the long procession and cavalcade—the "Everett Barge" with its fairy crew—the fire engines—the brilliant escort of the Boston Cadets commanded by Col. Thomas C. Amory—the march through various streets—the long ranks of children belonging to the schools, each sex in tasteful uniform, a beautiful feature in the ceremonies—and then the great tent on Meeting House Hill, formed a panorama of beautiful pictures amidst the sylvan scenery of time-hallowed Dorchester. In the line of march were seen the house where EDWARD EVERETT, orator of the day, was born, decorated with an arch supported by pillars on which was inscribed, THE SCHOLAR AND STATESMAN, together with the date of his birth, entrance at College, and the numerous offices he had sustained ; and in another place the house, conspicuous for its banner and motto, where he learnt his A B C. The houses on the route were gracefully ornamented, especially the mansion of Gov. Gardner, on the top of which waved a lofty banner, while on a handsome arch in front stood out OLD MASSACHUSETTS AND UNION FOREVER. Over the Pavilion was also an

arch with the inscription, DORCHESTER WAS SETTLED IN 1630, and on
the pillars the names of sixteen settlers.

Among those whom the merry bells of Dorchester had summoned
on that glorious day, were Gov. Henry J. Gardner, who was born
there, James Walker, D.D., Pres. of Harvard University, Hon. Charles
Francis Adams, Hon. Rufus Choate, and Hon. Peter Cooper of New
York, Rev. Edward Everett Hale, Judges and other personages.

About two thousand ladies and gentlemen sat down at the banquet,
in the tent, in which were various mottoes congenial to the occasion;
one of which it would be unjust to omit. It was the inscription on
an arch, decked with evergreens and flowers, in front of his seat :

MARSHALL P. WILDER,
President of the Day.

" Blessed is he that turneth the waste places into a garden and maketh the wilderness to
blossom as a rose."

The following is selected from the President's Address :

" The soil on which we have assembled is consecrated by the recollection of devoted
patriotism, and is sanctified by the sacrifices of a noble ancestry. Before us roll the
waters which bore on their bosom the good ship Mary and John, freighted with the first
settlers of Dorchester. Here were the homes of John Maverick, John Warham, Richard
Mather and their godly associates. Here and around us, were the homes of Hancock, of
Warren, of Prescott, of the Adamses, and other illustrious patriots, who struck some of
the first and heaviest blows for freedom, and who consecrated themselves at the altar
of liberty by a baptism of fire and blood. Within our view are Dorchester Heights and
Bunker Hill, those everlasting sentinels, which have guarded with sleepless vigilance
Massachusetts Bay, in times of awful peril; and there, faithful to their trust, they will
stand forever.

" We also rejoice in the presence of our neighbors from the various towns which have
arisen from the original Dorchester settlement, for the promptness and cordiality with
which they have responded to our invitation, especially to the citizens of Boston, a part of
whose territory was once the ' old cow pasture ' of the Dorchester settlers. [Laughter and
applause.] Ladies and Gentlemen, I intend no reflection upon the Queen city of New England, and she needs no encomium from me. There she stands in her proud pre-eminence,
like ancient Rome upon her Capitoline hill. As we gaze at her forest of masts, her crowded and busy marts, her princely dwellings and institutions, and consider her wealth, intelligence and power, we may indulge in a little ancestral pride, for we cannot forget that in
the Colonial tax of 1633, Dorchester paid £80, or one fifth of the whole tax, while Boston
paid but £48; and that as history informs us, ' Dorchester was the greatest town in New
England,' but that Boston was too small to contain many people."

Mr. Everett's oration gave universal satisfaction. When the orator
in imagination ascended the Heights of Dorchester, and Washington
seemed to stand before us on the eve of his first great victory, a thrill
of applause burst forth. But there is no applause like the profound attention of an immense audience. For two hours he held the
charmed mind of the assembly under the sway of his eloquence.

On the 4th of July, 1861, the patriotic citizens of Dorchester assembled to raise a new national flag. Mr. Wilder presided on the occasion, and at the close of his speech remarked:

"Thus shall we bind these States together in one great circle of life and love—make them one in inheritance, one in interest, one in destiny—a happy, prosperous and united people, whose love of liberty, self government and progress shall be the wonder of the world. Hold on to the Union! and as sure as yonder sun shall set beyond these distant hills, to rise another morning, so sure shall the clouds of gloom that now overshadow our beloved country be succeeded by a brighter and fairer hereafter. Raise high, then, the flag of our Union! Unfurl it, ye winds of heaven! and long as the bright canopy above shall continue to reflect the wisdom, goodness and power of an Almighty Hand, so long may our glorious banner, not one star fallen or blotted from its horizon, continue to be the emblem of the peace, prosperity and unity of this great Republic!"

Mr. W. had little desire for political life; his favorite pursuits were more congenial to his taste. But, in 1839, he was induced to serve as Representative to the State Legislature for the town of Dorchester, for one term. The next year he was elected a member of Gov. Briggs's Council, the year following a Senator, and in the organization of the Legislature, for that year, he was chosen President of the Senate. The remarks at the close of the session offered by Judge Pliny Merrick, a member from Worcester county, on proposing the customary vote of thanks, proved that his services were well appreciated, even by his political opponents.

"I rise to perform," said he, "one of the last and most grateful duties which devolve upon us, before our adjournment announces a final separation. Though composed of different political parties, we have not often been led, in the course of our deliberations, to divide according to our political relations; however we have differed from each other in debate, or in the votes we have given, no acerbity of temper has at any time been manifested; but a spirit of conciliation has always prevailed to quench every feeling of animosity. To this harmonious action no one has offered larger contributions than have been derived from the untiring assiduity and uniform urbanity of our presiding officer. I therefore take great pleasure in offering the resolution which I hold in my hand, and which I am confident will secure the cordial assent and unanimous approbation of the Senate."

But when the "Constitutional Union Party" was formed in Washington, the National Committee, of which the Hon. J. J. Crittenden was Chairman, selected Mr. Wilder as the member for New England. It devolved on him to call a meeting of the citizens of Massachusetts. They chose delegates, of which he was Chairman, to the Baltimore Convention, in which John Bell was nominated as candidate for the office of President of the United States, and Edward Everett for that of Vice President. The result of the election is a matter of history. It is well known to all his friends, that on every occasion, and in all his public addresses, he has been a warm supporter of the Union.

Nor should it be forgotten that he is a member of the Masonic Fraternity. He was made a Mason in Charity Lodge, No. 18, of Troy, N. H. in 1823, when he was 25 years old. He was afterwards exalted in the Royal Arch Chapter, Cheshire, No. 4, and since his residence in Boston he has become a Knight Templar and member of the Boston Encampment; and was, in 1861, Deputy Grand Master in the Grand Lodge of Massachusetts, and assisted in laying the corner-stone of the new City Hall on December 22, 1862. He also re-ceived the Thirty-third and Last Degree of the Ancient, Accepted Scottish Right in the Supreme Council of the Northern Jurisdiction of the United States, at Boston, in 1863.

In the great Roll of Brethren who, December 31, 1831, subscribed the " Declaration of the Free Masons of Boston and its vicinity," which was a faithful exponent of their loyalty to government and alle-giance to the laws, as well as their solemn denial of the unjust charges of their enemies, I find his name by the side of the Rev. Asa Eaton, D.D., Rev. Thaddeus Mason Harris, D.D., Rev. Edward T. Taylor, Rev. E. M. P. Wells, D.D., and other eminent clergymen and citizens. This famous document, written by Charles W. Moore, Grand Secre-tary of G. Lodge of Massachusetts, was signed by six thousand faithful, upright, unwavering Masons of New England.

Mr. Wilder, on the 29th of August, 1833, in his second marriage, was united to Miss Abigail Baker, daughter of Capt. David Baker, of Franklin, Massachusetts — a lady of education, accomplish-ments and piety. She died of a decline, April 4, 1854, leaving six children. He was married to her sister, Sept. 8, 1855—Miss Julia Baker — a lady admirably qualified to make his dwelling happy and comfort him during a long sickness brought on by over exertion and exposure, from which he is now slowly recovering. No man has been more blessed in his domestic life ; and would delicacy permit the writer to draw aside that sacred veil which shuts out the great world from the privacy of home, I know not where there would be a more pleasing picture exhibited than in the peace and content-ment of this happy family. Moreover, whether at home or abroad,

he is never idle ; his mind is at work in some favorite pursuit. Devoting his leisure hours to his pen, he has already filled several large
volumes with descriptions and delineations of fruits proved under his
own inspection. This has been the work of many years, and it is
hoped the public may hereafter have the benefit of his investigations.

His ability as a presiding officer needs no comment, as the flourishing condition of numerous societies under his administration evince
the high estimation with which his labors were invariably regarded.
He has often been called to the chair on various occasions not
before mentioned. He was President of the Massachusetts School of
Agriculture, incorporated in 1858, and about to be located at Springfield, which had offered the town farm and buildings with large sub-
scriptions for this object, when it was superseded by an Act of Congress granting lands to each State for an Agricultural College. He
presided over the Board of Agriculture at Washington, for two weeks,
when it was summoned by the Secretary of the Interior in 1859. Nor
should it be omitted, that in 1859, he presided at the first public meeting
called in Boston, in regard to a collocation of the institutions on the
Back Bay lands, where the splendid edifices of the Boston Society of
Natural History and the Massachusetts Institute of Technology now
stand. He was Chairman of the general Committee who petitioned for
these lands, and of the last Society he is one of the Vice Presidents.
The progress of the Technological Institute has been wonderful ; for it is
not only the possessor of a magnificent building, 150 feet by 90, where
seven years ago a deep tide ebbed and flowed, but has become a College, under William B. Rogers, LL.D., with fifteen professors and one
hundred and thirty students. Its lands, buildings and funds are
valued at above $600,000, and it seems destined to sow the seeds of
knowledge broadcast over the land. He is a member of many Horticultural and Agricultural Societies in this and foreign lands ; such
as the Royal Horticultural Societies of Paris, of Frankfort on the Main,
and the Pomological Society Van Mons of Belgium, by which he was
appointed a Commissioner for America ; and he has been a member
of the Massachusetts Agricultural Club twenty-seven years. He was
also one of the twelve Representative men, appointed to receive the
Prince of Wales at the banquet given him in Boston, in 1860.

The life of Mr. Wilder is a striking instance of what a single individual may accomplish by indomitable perseverance and the concentration of his intellectual powers upon one grand object—that of raising the standard of Terraculture in public opinion. No ordinary talent, no turn of mere good fortune, could ever have placed him in the high position he has attained as a public benefactor. For we must take into view the difficulties and obstacles which in private life impede every great and noble enterprise. One alone can do but little. He needs help. He must stir up the public mind to favor his plans ; he must enlist men of congenial temperament and willing to make some sacrifice, to unite with him in the cause. This necessarily leads to the formation of societies with rules and regulations ; and every society must have a head to plan, to arrange, to direct its operations. Nor is this all. The presiding officer should be the soul of the association, ever remembering that in this age of progress, societies are the instruments, but the master-spirit at the head is the great agitator of all improvement ; as the Poet affirmed long ago on a more exalted occasion :

" Mens agitat molem et magno se copore miscet."
Mind moves the mass, and the great body fills.

He who presides, therefore, should not only be a workman, but possess a winning manner, knowledge, talents and eloquence to draw toward him, on all public occasions, our most distinguished men. He must spare no expense, shrink from no labor ; he must confine his efforts to no narrow section, but like the eagle from his aerie look abroad and embrace the whole country in his glance, until a nation feels the importance of his movements, and the wisest and most enlightened citizens aid him with their influence, and the yeomanry of the land, wherever his exhibitions are held, surround him with their presence.

Such was the subject of this memoir, who was President of many great and prosperous associations—the Massachusetts Horticultural, the American Pomological, the Norfolk County, and the United States Agricultural Societies. An appeal to the numerous and splendid exhibitions already described will justify the remarks of the writer. Yet, should any reader think them too highly colored, the conclusion of this memoir must remove all doubt.

At a quarterly meeting of the Massachusetts Horticultural Society, April 1, 1863, a letter was received from Charles O. Whitmore, Esq., a zealous patron of the Society and one of the eminent merchants of Boston. On presenting a fine marble Bust of Mr. Wilder, he remarks :

"For more than thirty years, Col. Wilder has been connected with this Society, and has not only given liberally of his money, but has devoted his time and influence to the furtherance of its objects. Beginning at a time when the importance of such a Society was not appreciated, and its objects seemed almost visionary, he has seen it gradually rising in public estimation, and exerting a constantly increasing influence among the land-holders of New England."

Having then stated that " he deserved the thanks of the Society " for having made such wise and prudent arrangements with the Mt. Auburn Cemetery Corporation, Mr. Whitmore observes :

" I need hardly add that Col. Wilder's connection with this Society is not his sole claim to public distinction. He has repeatedly been called upon to occupy offices of trust and responsibility, and has ably discharged the duties devolved upon him. As a merchant he has given a notable example of integrity and ability, and his personal character needs no encomium from us, who have been intimately associated with him. The particular interest, however, which Col. Wilder has always evinced in the success of this and kindred societies, renders this a peculiarly fitting place to present such a memorial." See *Am. Gardener's Magazine*, Vol. xxix. p. 201-2.

The following Resolution was then adopted :

" *Resolved*, That as members of the Massachusetts Horticultural Society, we are highly gratified in being able to add to our valuable collection of ornamentations, so fine a marble Bust of one who for more than thirty years has been an active member, patron, friend and constant benefactor of our Society ; for eight years its President, in which time Horticultural Hall was built — to whose conservative, conciliatory and wise influence the Society is largely indebted for that amicable settlement with the Mount Auburn Cemetery Corporation, from which a large income has already been received, and by which a perpetual revenue is to accrue to its funds. Nor would we, as members of this Society, be unmindful, that in thus honoring our own fellow citizen, we are paying deserved homage to one who has richly earned for himself a national reputation by serving the United States Agricultural Society six years as its efficient President, and also as President of the American Pomological Society for the last twelve years, which office he still fills."

Mr. Wilder is about to leave for Europe, having been appointed by the American Pomological and the U. S. Agricultural Societies Commissioner to represent these institutions at the Paris World's Fair and other exhibitions in Europe during the present year. He will take with him the cordial wishes of his many friends for the perfect recovery of his health.

8

Since the foregoing was written, an annual meeting of the Norfolk Agricultural Society was held at Dedham, on the 27th of March, 1867, when the following Resolutions were unanimously passed, and published in the Dedham Gazette.

" *Whereas*, it is understood that the President of this Society—the Hon. Marshall P. Wilder—is about to embark on a voyage to Europe, for the recovery of his health ; and

" *Whereas*, a deep sense of obligation to him, and a warm interest in the chief object of his visit abroad, are felt by the Society ;

" Therefore, *Resolved*, That an assurance of our grateful remembrance of his services in behalf of the Society, and of our most earnest desire for the complete recovery of his health, his safety while abroad, and his speedy return to his native land, be, and is hereby, tendered to our beloved President, the Hon. Marshall P. Wilder.

" *Resolved*, That this Society constitute Mr. Wilder as their Representative at the coming World's Exposition at Paris, and as their Delegate to all kindred associations which he may visit during his sojourn abroad."

"Mr. Wilder, in brief and fitting terms, acknowledged the repeated tokens of respect and confidence which he had received from the Society, and his heartfelt appreciation of the personal regard of the members as expressed in the resolutions."

GENEALOGY.

This contains the lineage of Mr. Wilder's family, arranged from the "Book of the Lockes;" the History of Hingham, by Hon. Solomon Lincoln; the History of Leominster, by Hon. David Wilder; and from other sources. It can be traced from Thomas Wilder, 1640: but the descent from Martha is not so sure. The name of Martha, according to Mr. Drake's investigations in England, to which we owe that exceedingly useful work, "The Founders of New England"—was in the list of passengers who came out in the ship *Confidence*, in 1638; from Shiplake, two miles south of Henley by the Thames. And the tradition in Hingham, is, that she had two sons with her, Edward and Thomas. Edward remained there and left two children, of whom there are numerous descendants; Thomas went to Charlestown, and afterwards to Lancaster. But the subject has been so fully examined by Mr. Lincoln, to whom the writer is indebted for a careful summary of the evidence, that there can be little doubt upon this subject.

I. MARTHA WILDER, widow, came from England, and according to Hingham records owned lands there in 1638; d. April 20, 1652.

II. Children of Martha[1] :—(1) Edward,[2] m. Elizabeth Eames, of Marshfield, lived in Hingham, leaving issue; d. Oct. 28, 1690. (2) THOMAS,[2] admitted to church, Charlestown, Jan. 1, 1640; Juryman, 1658; moved to Lancaster July 1, 1659; m. Anna ——, who d. 1692; he d. Oct. 23, 1667.

III. Children of Thomas[2] :—(1) Thomas,[3] b. 1641. (2) John.[3] (3) NATHANIEL,[3] killed by Indians at Lancaster, July, 1704.

IV. Children of Nathaniel[3] :—(1) Jonathan.[4] (2) Nathaniel.[4] (3) EPHRAIM,[4] who was wounded in Indian fight at Lancaster, 1707; d. 1769, aged 94. (4) Oliver.[4]

V. Children of EPHRAIM[4] :—(1) EPHRAIM,[5] b. 1702, d. March, 1770.

VI. Children of Ephraim[5] :—(1) Capt. EPHRAIM,[6] b. July 8, 1733; m. April 3, 1755, Lucretia, sister of Samuel Locke, D.D.; she was b. Nov. 5, 1733, and died Dec. 29, 1816, aged 83; he was Representative some years from Sterling; d. Jan. 29, 1805, aged 72. (2) Manassah.[6] (3) William.[6]

VII.   Children of Capt. Ephraim W.[6]:—(1) Ephraim,[7] b. April 29, 1756 ; m. Hannah Reed, about 1778. (2) Timothy,[7] b. Dec. 2, 1759 ; m. Eunice Osgood, 1783. (3) Lucretia,[7] b. June 19, 1761 ; m. Ebenezer Pope, 1780. (4) Elizabeth,[7] b. July 22, 1763 ; m. Joseph Kendall, Feb. 15, 1814, who d. Nov. 1, 1835. She d. without issue March 9, 1852, aged 89. (5) Rebecca,[7] b. Sept. 7, 1765, d. May, 1766. (6) Joel,[7] b. July 7, 1767 ; m. Lucy Kendall, 1789. (7) Josiah,[7] b. July 16, 1770 ; m. Susan Carlton, April 11, 1801. (8) Harrison,[7] b. Feb. 11, 1774 ; m. Keziah Powers, Jan. 3, 1803. (9) SAMUEL LOCKE,[7] b. March 14, 1778 ; m. Anna Sherwin, May 20, 1797, dau. of Jonathan Sherwin, of Rindge, grandfather of Thomas Sherwin, Principal of the Boston High School. She was b. Dec. 31, 1778, d. Feb. 5, 1851, aged 72. He removed to Rindge, 1794 ; d. April 7, 1863, aged 85.

VIII.   Children of Samuel Locke W.[7] : (1) MARSHALL PINCKNEY,[8] b. Sept. 22, 1798 ; m. 1st, Tryphosa, dau. of Stephen Jewett, of Rindge, Dec. 31, 1820 ; b. Dec. 27, 1799, d. on a visit there, July 31, 1831 ; 2d, m. August 29, 1833, Abigail, dau. of Capt. David Baker, of Franklin, Mass. She was b. Aug. 4, 1810, d. at Aiken, S. C. of consumption, April 4, 1854 ; 3d, m. Sept. 8, 1855, Julia, sister of Abigail Baker, b. Oct. 21, 1821. (2) Eurydice,[8] b. July 13, 1801, d. Jan. 9, 1818. (3) Frederic Adolphus,[8] b. April 16, 1804 ; m. Apphia Tyler, Jan. 28, 1828. (4) Mary Ann,[8] b. April 1, 1806 ; m. Rev. Albert B. Camp, Feb. 3, 1829, d. Dec. 25, 1830. (5) Nancy,[8] b. Nov. 10, 1809, d. Feb. 23, 1830. (6) Josiah,[8] b. Oct 31, 1813 ; m. Elizabeth F. Fosdick, May 13, 1835, d. April 27, 1853. (7) Mersilvia,[8] b. June 18, 1816 ; m. Stephen B. Sherwin, April 16, 1835. He d. Dec. 14, 1861. (8) Eurydice Augusta, b. Jan. 28, 1819. (9) Samuel Locke,[8] b. Jan. 9, 1822 ; m. 1st, Anna[8] L. Silsby, Oct. 15, 1845, who d. Jan. 18, 1856 ; 2d, m. Lorania L. Tuttle, Sept., 1857.

IX.   Children of Col. Marshall P. W.[8] :—(1) by his 1st wife: Marshall Pinckney,[9] merchant, b. Jan. 15, 1822 ; m. E. Clara, dau. of James C. Churchill, of Portland, Me., July 17, 1844; he d. at Dorchester, Dec. 29, 1854. (2) Eurydice,[9] b. June 11, 1823, d. at Rindge, Oct. 4, 1824. (3) Nancy Jewett,[9] b. Feb. 19, 1825 ; m. Dec. 28, 1858, Rev. Andrew Bigelow, D.D., now of Boylston. (4) Lucius Icilius,[9] b. Oct. 27, 1826, merchant, New Orleans. (5) Maria Louisa,[9] b. July 28,

1828; m. Ambrose Wager, of Rhinebeck, N. Y., Sept. 26, 1850, and d. there of consumption, June 2, 1852. (6) William Henry,[9] b. July 15, 1830, d. Aug. 31, 1831. (7) By his second wife: Abbie Tryphosa,[9] b. May 22, 1834; m. Nov. 10, 1859, Wm. Wallace, merchant of Boston. (8) William Henry,[9] b. March 17, 1836, merchant; m. Oct. 17, 1861, Hannah, sister of William Wallace. (9) Sarah Jane,[9] b. Sept. 29, 1841, d. July 28, 1858. (10) Samuel Locke,[9] b. Oct. 2, 1843, d. Oct. 5, 1853. (11) Jemima Richardson,[9] b. June 30, 1845. (12) Grace Sherwin,[9] b. April 23, 1851. (13) By last wife: Edward Baker,[9] b. Nov. 17, 1857. (14) Marshall Pinckney,[9] b. Oct. 3, 1860.

X. Children of Maria Louisa[9] and Ambrose Wager:—(1) Henry Wilder,[10] b. April, 1852, d. July, 1852.

Children of Abbie[9] and William Wallace:—(1) Ida,[10] b. April 22, 1861, d. April 5, 1863. (2) Belle,[10] b. Sept. 8, 1862. (3) Annie,[10] b. Sept. 8, 1864. (4) Edith,[10] b. Dec. 6, 1865. (5) Jennie Wilder,[10] b. March 6, 1867.

Children of William H. Wilder[9]:—(1) Alice,[10] b. Nov. 5, 1862. (2) Lizzie,[10] b. Nov. 27, 1864. (3) William Henry, Jr.,[10] b. March 31, 1867.

————

The subjoined letter of the Hon. SOLOMON LINCOLN contains the document referred to in the Genealogy.

WILDER.

The Hingham traditionary account of the family of Wilder as published by me, in 1827, in the History of Hingham, was that "a widow by the name of Wilder came out of England with two boys, her only children, having before their departure disposed of their entailed estate; and she never would disclose to her son Edward, who settled with her in Hingham, nor to any other person that we know of, the name of the place in England from which they came. Our ancestors have not left us any uniform tradition respecting the other boy, some of them supposing that he must have been the Wilder from whom descended the families of that name in Lancaster and its vicinity," &c.

This account of the family tradition was given to me by Joseph Wilder and Joshua Wilder, of Hingham, forty years since. They were intelligent men.

The Lancaster tradition, published by Joseph Willard, Esq., in his History of Lancaster (*Worcester Magazine*, Sept. 1826), was that Thomas Wilder, the first of that name in this country, came from Lancaster in England, that he settled in Hingham, had four sons, that one son remained in Hingham, from whom are descended all of the name of Wilder in that town and vicinity," &c.

The Leominster tradition, as published by Hon. David Wilder, in his history of that town, in 1853, was stated as follows: "At an early date (previous to 1638) a widow by the name of Martha Wilder (Wyelder) came from Lancaster in England, to Hingham in Massachusetts. She was accompanied by two sons, Thomas and Edward—the latter remaining in Hingham, and the former, after having resided some years in Charlestown, removed to Lancaster in the County of Worcester, July 1, 1659, and must then have been about forty years of age. He had three sons: Thomas, born 1641, John, and Nathaniel," &c.

Samuel G. Drake, in his Result of Researches published in 1860, p. 59, has the following in the list of passengers in the ship Confidence, "C C tonnes," gone for New England in April, 1638.

"Martha Wildᵉ of Shiplocke in Oxfordsᵉ *Spinster.*
Mary Wildᵉ *her Daughter."*

Mr. Drake, in a note, says "*Shiplake,* by the Thames, two miles South of Henly." I find that Moule, in his English Counties, vol. ii. page 70, describes Shiplake—"3 miles S. of Henley, contains 101 houses and 528 inhabitants," in Oxfordshire. Moule's English Counties was published in London, 1837.

Hingham Records show grants of land to "Widow Wilder" in 1638, viz.: a House Lot, Planting Lot, Great Lot, and Salt marsh. There is a grant of Salt marsh (recorded on same page) to Edward Wilder without date—and on the next page, under date of 1647, another grant of Salt marsh to Edward Wilder, perhaps the same as the foregoing.

By other Hingham Records, it is well established that Widow Martha Wilder was the mother of Edward.

Widow Martha Wilder died April 20, 1652. Edward, freeman 1644, married Elizabeth Eames of Marshfield, "before 1654" says Reuben Hersey of Hingham, in his private record; had sons John, Ephraim, Isaac and Jabez, and four daughters. He died Oct. 18, 1690. His widow died June 9, 1692. Hingham Records give a full account of the descendants of Edward Wilder. A Summary of the record is contained in Lincoln's History of Hingham.

In a correspondence held with Hon. David Wilder of Leominster, in 1860, the traditionary accounts of Leominster and Hingham were the subjects of inquiry, and the result seemed to be that Martha Wilder of Hingham 1638, was the mother of Thomas and Edward. We do not find any evidence as to the time when Thomas and Edward came to this country, except from tradition. The place from which she came was evidently Shiplake in Oxfordshire, and not Lancaster, as Lancaster (N. E.) tradition states. It is not uncommon that the descendants of an ancient family conjecture that the name of the home of their ancestors was given to the place of their settlement.

The fact that Mary Wilder came with her mother neither proves nor disproves that she had other children who came afterwards. The name of Mary Wilder, if she remained unmarried, would not appear in our Records except at her decease.

There was a Mary Wilder born in Hingham in 1668, supposed to be one of Edward's daughters. This is probably a correct supposition, and would indicate that Mary was a family name, being that of her aunt.

It may also be remarked, as pertinent to the discussion of the question whether Thomas of Charlestown and Edward of Hingham were related, that they each had a daughter Mary, and a son John, and Ephraim appears to have been a family name in both branches. So also are Thomas, Nathaniel and Ebenezer.

So far as I have been able to collect evidence relating to the history of the first settlers in Hingham and Lancaster of the name of Wilder, the evidence from tradition, corrected by authentic records, is confirmatory of the opinion that Thomas and Edward were brothers. A full account of the descendants of Edward, of Hingham, can be given if desired. They are numerous, and their names would fill a volume. The historians of Lancaster, Leominster and Leicester, seem to have the means of giving a full and satisfactory account of their branch of the family.

But perhaps I have in these notes by way of preliminary inquiry given enough to suggest the course of examination for more evidence of the history of the race in England. The records of Shiplake may throw some light on the subject; and possibly those in Lancaster, England, may be worthy of examination, although I doubt whether the tradition that the family came from that place is sufficiently fortified by more authentic records.

SOLOMON LINCOLN.

Hingham, January 26, 1867.

www.ingramcontent.com/pod-product-compliance
Lightning Source LLC
Chambersburg PA
CBHW030855260626
47169CB00008B/2552